The Zombie War

Battle for Britain

Contents

Authors Note

It had never been my intention to write a book about the Zombie War. In the years of peace that followed the darkest period in human history, a time when the light of civilisation was in danger of being extinguished by the creatures that even today defy explanation and understanding, I felt it was somehow undignified and demeaning to be telling stories of those that had died.

My moment of epiphany came when I was covering the Olsen Review that took place some five years after the end of the war. At the time, I was a journalist for a well-known broadsheet newspaper and reported on many of the key events during and after the war. During the inquest, one piece of information caught my attention. A sociologist had stated in her report, that in another thirty years' time many of the Zombie War generation, those that had been there at the start of the conflict, would be dead. My first reaction was, of course, one of concern for my own longevity. However, the more I thought about it the more I realised that importance of recording the survivor's tales for posterity.

I approached my editor with the idea of doing a series of human interest pieces to tell those stories and thankfully she allowed me a limited run in the Sunday edition. They were a great success, with people clamouring for more. It seemed that the stories had ignited a fire in the people of Britain to know more of others' experiences.

I was approached by the National Archive and commissioned to construct a series of survivor's accounts to be recorded for posterity. Armed with funding, an assistant to write up the interviews and a Royal Writ to go where I please and talk to who I wished, I set off on a long and emotional journey. It took me three years but the product was many thousands of interviews written and stored in the National Archive in London and all of it open to the public.

While I was understandably proud of my work I felt that it was still somewhat impersonal and that while it was free to all to view it was not practical for many people to travel to London. There were already numerous biographies, official histories, magazine articles and documentaries in the public domain telling different aspects of The War and there is, of course, the Government's Olsen Review which had sought out the cold hard facts. To me, there was nothing that filled the gap, no overarching manuscript to bring these great stories of individual struggle together into a coherent tale.

It is my hope that this book can help to fill that gap and contribute to keeping these fascinating stories alive. Human history is after all the stories of people and their actions. Without the personal aspect then history loses its context and I feel that the history of Britain would be lessened without them.

The Zombie War is without a doubt the most devastating and at the same time important event in human history. In my mind, it is the first truly global war that has affected every single corner of this planet and every single person living on it. No war has brought about the profound political, social, economic, environmental and psychological changes that this one has. Countries have changed shape, political direction and religion. Some have been weakened and some have come out stronger.

Britain has been irrevocably changed in the past twenty years. In some ways, the country is a better and stronger place but in others, we have been weakened almost to the point of breaking. Life expectancy and the standard of living are a shadow of their pre-war levels but Britons are a stronger, more unified people with a more focused understanding of our place in the world. To say The War has made the country a better place would be an insult to all those that have died but it has brought people together in the way a common threat always does. It would not be unfair to say that the sunset on the empire many years before the war, even if it took a long time for many people to realise it. But in the darkness of The War Britain rediscovered its self-worth and strove to create a better, fairer and more equal world that will hopefully ensure peace for many generations.

It is my ardent hope that this book stands as a testament to those who lived and died through the many years of struggle. My heartfelt thanks to all those who consented to be interviewed and my apologies to those whose stories did not make it into this edition. Special thanks are due to the curator of the National Archives who made this journey possible in the first place.

Tom Holroyd

WRITING ON THE WALL

First Contact

Westminster, London

Mike Hodgson is not the stereotypical SAS soldier depicted in films, books and television. At first glance, one could almost pass over the slightly built, unassuming man sitting quietly at the corner table of a London pub. Mike actually contacted me for this interview, having heard that I was interviewing soldiers who had served in Afghanistan during the first phases of the war.

I was a career soldier. I joined the Army at 17 to get away from a shit life in a London council estate and signed on with the Parachute Regiment. It was a quiet time for the Army as this was before Iraq and Afghanistan properly kicked off, all we really had was Northern Ireland tours and the Balkans. I had joined for some action so after three years of service I decided to give Selection a go.

When people think of the SAS they think of steely-eyed dealers of death swinging through windows and killing the bad guys. Muscled supermen who deal death to the King's enemies. It's all a load of shit cooked up by the media, TV programs and all the ex-Regiment lads who write crappy novels that give away all our tactics for a pile of cash. Can't really say as I blame them though; given the amount of money thrown at some mates of mine over the years.

The truth is that most people wouldn't recognise someone from the SAS if they were stood next to them. We are all just ordinary blokes who have been through some extraordinary things and that's what Selection identifies and picks out in people. Yeah, it's physically demanding but it is the mental side that gets you. Walking mile after mile in shit Welsh weather, over what seems like never-ending hills with no end in sight, that's what breaks people and that's what the Regiment look for in its soldiers. It is the ability to keep going no matter what, to look at that hill and say "Fuck you! You're not going to beat me". It was this mental robustness that built the legend and made us so well placed to carry out the job we did in the war.

Can you tell me about Afghanistan?

The Regiment was really in their element there.

We had done some good work in Iraq targeting the insurgent hierarchy and the bomb makers and helped bring things to a much faster conclusion but it was in Afghanistan where we really came into our own. Our main role was as a rapid strike force and we were very, very busy. A bit of Intelligence would come in that some high-value target was crossing the border from Pakistan and would be at some location at a certain time. We would head out and raid the place to either kill or capture the target.

I just want to be clear though; we always went out with the intent to capture and would only kill if the bastard wouldn't play nicely. We weren't like some units that would just drop into a village and brass the place up looking for one man. It was always quick, quiet and hopefully blood free.

One day we get a call from the ISAF (**International Security Assistance Force)** Int Cell in Kabul. A source in Pakistan had told them a senior member of the insurgency was crossing the border and would be staying in a village near Peshawar. There were no American Special Forces units available and could we go and have a crack at him? Of course, the boys had been getting a bit restless by then. The vast majority of British troops had pulled out along with over half the Americans and things had been fairly quiet with the Afghans sorting out their own problems. The only thing going on was the increased reports of refugee traffic coming across the border from China and India but even that was only worthy of a small sentence in the nightly Int brief.

Anyway, the Boss jumped at the chance for a bit of work.

Twelve of us jumped onto a C-130 and shot off North. The plan was for a simple night raid, usual format; parachute out near the village, patrol in, raid the target house, secure the package, get picked up by the helicopters and back in time for breakfast. We had done it a thousand times before and had no reason to doubt this time would be different.

It was about half an hour's flight from Kabul to the target village, a shitty little place with no name, it wasn't even marked on most maps and the only way we found it was through satellite photos. It was a tiny hamlet with twenty to thirty houses that sat in an east-west running valley. All the Int pointed to it being a traditional route for people smuggling, drugs and gun running over the mountains.

We landed about 2 km to the east of the village, stashed the 'chutes and began our patrol in. As soon as we hit the main track running into the village we knew something wasn't right. We started to come across abandoned vehicles, some with smashed windows. Blood stains were on the ground and around the doors and there was the odd bullet casing scattered on the ground. There was a flatbed truck stuck in a drainage ditch by the side of the road. It had one of those raised boxes on the back and there were these holes punched in the side like someone had been keeping an animal in there. The doors of the box were hanging off the hinges and there was fresh blood on the ground around it. Our first thought was that some dumb bastard had been smuggling a tiger or something across the border and it must have gotten free and run rampant before fucking off.

We cast around, looking for whatever ground sign we could through the Night Vision Goggles and soon came across these strange tracks that looked human but had a weird dragging gait like the person was lame. The tracks, about five sets, headed off in the direction of the village. We cracked on, definitely starting to get a little bit spooked by now, and got within 500m of the village. It was at this point that one of the lads commented over the net that there we no dogs barking. Afghans would always tether dogs in a

8

ring around a village to act as early warning but there was nothing. There was a slight rise in front of us, so we all went to ground and crawled forward till we could see the village.

It was a fucking mess, doors smashed off their hinges, blood splashed up the walls and pooled on the floor. There were bodies on the ground and we could see bullet holes pockmarking the walls and doors. Nothing was moving.

The Boss gave us the order to move forward. We picked ourselves up and started to patrol carefully forward over the field towards the first compound. Pretty much as soon as I got up I was back on my face again as I tripped over something. I had found out what had happened to the guard dogs. They had been ripped apart and half eaten.

As we got closer to the compound we found the first body, a man again ripped apart. It was obvious from the way he was facing, the rusty AK by his side and a pile of shell casings at his feet that he had been firing at something coming down the track from the direction of the abandoned vehicles.

We guessed that a group of people, maybe five had come down the track towards the first compound and been smelt by the dog, the dog had gone ape-shit and woken its master. The dog then got torn apart before the man had come out and started shooting. He had evidently hit naff all and then been killed himself.

All this was surmised very quickly and quietly before the Boss decided we would continue with the original mission and try and grab our target. We moved off very slowly and quietly keeping one eye on the tracks and one on the road ahead. As we passed each compound the tracks would move straight toward the door and then into the compound. In the courtyards, all we could see was blood, torn up bodies and shattered doors.

We reached the target compound and found the door hanging off the hinges; the courtyard looked like a fucking slaughterhouse. I've never seen or smelt anything like it.

Our target had evidently overnighted here and brought a large bodyguard with him, fuck all good it did him though. There were ten or twelve men scattered around the courtyard and I do mean scattered, they had all been facing the door and they were all in pieces. The compound wall around the door looked like it had been used for target practice and there were droplets of this brownish goo scattered around the doorway and all over the ground. We moved through the courtyard and started in amongst the bodies looking for our target. Most of them had been torn apart and partly eaten but there were two that were whole except for having their heads blown off. It looked as if these were our mystery attackers as they were riddled with bullets and were facing towards the bodyguards.

We fanned out to secure the compound with one team clearing the buildings. I watched a mate of mine duck into a doorway and then pile back out again vomiting. I didn't see what he did, as I was guarding the door to the courtyard but heard from him later that he had found the target, or what was left of him. It seems that he had locked himself in the storeroom and then shot himself in the head. Something or as was becoming more and more possible, someone, had then broken in and partially eaten him.

I should have been looking outwards for any signs of trouble, should have been checking my arcs but I was more interested in seeing what was going on behind me. So fucking unprofessional!

Anyway, I heard a low moan and this shuffling sound behind me. I spun around and came face to face with one of the attackers, fucking nearly shat myself.

Have you ever seen a Ghoul through a night sight? There is something about the eyes after they turn, they get glazed over and all scratched up because they don't blink. It gives them that dead, grey look but it also reflects the moonlight. It also has the wonderful side effect of making it seem like their eyes glow in the dark. If ever you need a cure for constipation to try that.

There were three of them about five meters away. They had just come around the corner of the next compound along and were heading straight for me. I yelled for the Boss and backed through the door which would force them to come at us one at a time. The Boss came running and looked through the door, even in the dark I could see his face drain of colour. He told us all to get as far back as possible as he wanted to try something.

Turns out the Boss was a big fan of horror movies, loved the old George A. Romero zombie flicks. He told me later he had had this nagging suspicion in the back of his mind all night but had dismissed it because it just couldn't be real. Now here it was shuffling and moaning towards us.

The Boss moved back from the door as the first one pushed through and raised his weapon. He fired off two shots straight into the heart. Nothing, it just took the hits and kept coming. He then raised his point of aim and shot it point blank in the head. The thing dropped like a sack of shit and didn't even twitch. He turned and trotted back to us, by then we had formed a firing line against the far wall of the compound and he told two of the lads to shoot them in the head. They let rip and the bastards dropped.

I think at that point one of the younger lads let loose with a "What the fuck!". The Boss was on the radio to Command trying to get them to understand what had happened and I don't think it was going well. He was yelling into the mike "Yes, fucking zombies, living dead, all that shit". He must have gotten through to someone who knew what we were talking about as we were told to stay put and secure the area. We were also told to make sure that all the corpses were properly dead. We were all a bit surprised by that last order until the Boss told us that in the movies people bitten by zombies can come back to life and needed to be shot in the head to stay dead. He ordered us to "secure" the village.

It was a pretty shitty half hour as we went from room to room and compound to compound slotting these corpses between the eyes. Some of them were even starting to reanimate by then. I tell you, nothing gets your heart pumping like looking down on a corpse preparing to pull the trigger when it suddenly opens its eyes and looks back.

By the time we had gotten back to the main compound the Boss had a G tied up, gagged and was sitting on its back as it squirmed underneath him. "Help" arrived pretty soon after that. Four Black Hawks and a Chinook landed outside the village and unloaded what looked like extras from a bio-hazard movie. They took control and hustled us onto a waiting Black Hawk. The last thing we saw as we headed off was the bound zombie being strapped to a medical gurney and carried onto the Chinook, behind us the village burned as they "sanitised" the area.

We spent the next month being de-briefed and tested by all manner of officers, doctors and civi's before we were allowed out and told not to discuss anything that had happened. We never saw the Boss after that. I heard rumours that he was sent back to the UK to brief the higher-ups and he became the lead officer for the Sanitation Teams. We were shipped out a couple of weeks later but by then it wasn't a secret any more, outbreaks were starting to pop up all over the world and people were starting to wake up to the reality. By then NATO had pretty much pulled out and gone home. I was on one of the last flights from Kabul with the British Ambassador and by then we were starting to see more and more refugees from China and India coming over the mountains.

It is ironic really, we spent all that time, money and blood trying to sort out Afghanistan. We had just gotten the country back on its feet and then The War happens and the whole thing goes down the throat of the Undead.

Guess it was always going to happen though. Afghanistan had spent its entire history as a thoroughfare for East and West; for trade, culture and empires and now it was the main thoroughfare for the infection to the rest of the world.

I hear there is not a lot left any more, what with the infected, the Asian mega swarms and of course the nuclear exchange between Iran and Pakistan. Shame really it was a beautiful country.

Intelligence Failure

Holkham Bay, Norfolk

I have been invited to the home of Sir James Marsden, the former Director General of the Royal Intelligence Service. A career intelligence officer, Sir John has spent a long and illustrious career in some of the most dangerous and unstable parts of the world. He was promoted to Director of the Security Intelligence Service or MI6 two years before The War and saw out the entire conflict in that role. He oversaw the merging of all the civilian and military intelligence services into the RIS and headed that organisation until his retirement last year. He is the image of the British establishment, impeccably dressed with an English Springer Spaniel resting at his feet. We are sitting on his patio enjoying a breathtaking view across the beach and out to the North Sea.

The problem with being in Intelligence is that you always feel unappreciated and ignored. Politicians and the general public always expect their Intelligence service to be able to predict every threat and plot focused on this country. The simple fact is we never could. We were damn good, don't get me wrong, we stopped more threats to this country than anyone will ever know but we were never funded to the degree we wished or given the legal freedom to effectively carry out our mission. I don't mean to sound like I am making excuses but it is important to set the scene. Before the war, before the panic, we were grossly unprepared for what was to come.

Intelligence back then had two main focuses; internal security which was the purview of MI5 and external threats which was the focus of MI6. I am sorry if that seems a bit broad brush but that is the easiest way to break it down.

I was focused outwards, on China, Russia, Iran, anyone who constituted a threat to this country and it was a bloody busy time. Did you know that in the years running up to The War there were more active intelligence agents in London than during the Cold War. Russia and China were busy trying to steal any secrets or technology that they could get their hands on and the Middle East was busy tearing itself apart.

The first hints that something was not quite right came from China. It all started when we got word of their Health and Safety sweeps. Our sources in the country and in the Communist Party were adamant that this was more than just the usual sweep up of dissidents and religious types. At the same time, we were getting regular tips and Signals Intelligence that all pointed to a security crackdown and mobilisation of troops. We got one intercept from an email conversation referring to bodies coming back to life and attacking people but no-one thought anything of it. Based on the intelligence available we concluded that it was a massive cover operation for a military move on Taiwan. All the evidence pointed to it and that's what we thought would happen. We were prepared for the call from the Americans asking us to go with them into the Taiwan Strait. It was a bloody huge intelligence failure.

Thank God though for insubordinate youngsters. A number of junior analysts were not convinced and despite their superiors ignoring their warnings, they kept digging. It was an inexcusable failure of leadership that these bright young people were ignored. It got so bad that they had to knock on my door and demand that I read their report. It was an eye-opener I can tell you.

It was a compilation of reports from various intelligence sources around the world; NGOs that were witnessing the increase in refugees and outbreaks firsthand; there was a report from Special Forces teams that were starting to see more incidents across Central Asia. All of it pointed to one implausible but inescapable conclusion; that we were dealing with a viral outbreak that killed its host before reanimating them as a flesh-eating zombie. I ordered all available resources to be diverted to dig into and identify the truth.

What action did you take?

I went straight to the Prime Minister. I demanded a meeting of his National Security Committee and briefed them myself.

What was the result?

To say I was laughed out of the room would be a bit harsh. The PM did not believe me and thought I was being sensational, most of his cabinet agreed with him. One even accused me of creating a threat to get a bigger budget. I almost punched him.

What happened next?

Well, the politicians filled out of the room still chuckling to themselves about paranoid intelligence chiefs and leaving me feeling impotent, embarrassed and frankly furious. It was then that I noticed the Chief of the Defence Staff (**Air Chief Marshal Sir Sebastian Benford GCB AFC**) was still there and looking at me in a rather worrying way. CDS asked me if I was serious, I replied that I was and this needed action now. He agreed that this issue warranted another look and we headed back to his office in the Ministry of Defence and had a very frank chat about what we felt needed to be done.

Was that the beginning of the Royalist movement?

Not at that point. I am sure one could argue that it was the first domino to fall but no the Royalist movement came much later and almost too late.

What happened at the meeting?

Well, CDS called in the three heads of the services and asked me to brief them. I went over the information again and we began to discuss the very real possibility of an outbreak in the UK as well as on a global scale. As the meeting went on, more and more people were called in, so much so that by the time we finished it was close to midnight and there were all the heads of the military and most of their staff all discussing the very real possibility of living dead overwhelming the country.

What decisions were made?

Well, there were no actual official decisions made, that required Ministerial approval you understand and it was clear from my meeting that morning that we were not going to get it. We had managed to thrash out a plan in outline to contain any outbreak in the mainland UK and what actions would need to be taken in the event of a full-blown pandemic. We did make one decision and that was to re-brief the PM and demand action.

What happened?

It was a full meeting of the Cabinet in Downing Street. The Chief of the Defence Staff, flanked by the head of the Army, Royal Navy and Royal Air Force stood in front of all those politicians and laid it out straight. He briefed the threat, the likely outcomes of an outbreak and then our plan to contain it.

What was the reaction?

The room was deathly silent, everyone waiting for the PM's reaction. He went ballistic. He was incensed that we would have the temerity to bring up a subject that he felt he had been very clear on. He did not consider this a credible threat and would not panic the public and waste "valuable political capital" on military scaremongering.

It was no secret that the PM did not like the military when he was Chancellor he had overseen the gradual reduction of military and security budgets and then as Prime Minister, he was again ignoring the clear and candid advice of his military staff because it would cost him points in the polls.

He went on like this for about five minutes getting redder and redder in the face until CDS finally lost his cool and slammed his hand down on the table. The PM had just spluttered something about "how dare we go against him like this!" CDS responded by saying;

"We dare Sir because it is the responsibility of those with power to protect those without. That is the role of the Armed Forces and that is what you are preventing us from doing. The first role of any Government is to protect its citizens and you are failing in that duty. If you will not take action then we will."

What was the Prime Minister's reaction?

He was less than pleased. There was more shouting and table slapping. A lot of the other ministers were joining in and we stood there and took it for a full three minutes before CDS turned to us and said "Gentlemen, we are done here. We have a country to serve." We all turned and walked out the door.

What was the fallout from the meeting?

You are the journalist, I am sure you remember.

Please, humour me.

Once the meeting was over we all walked back across Whitehall to the Ministry of Defence and waited for the axe to fall. We were not disappointed I can tell you. About ten minutes later there were demands for resignations, demands for apologies, in that order, the Secretary of State for Defence came in and demanded to know what we thought we were up too. "Our job" was the terse reply before he was shown the door.

Fairly soon after that, the media got wind of the fact that there had been a serious falling out between the military and Government. The Spin Doctors went into overdrive, the

MOD press office practically melted, there were recriminations and accusations from both sides and hanging over all of this was that fact that no one could say what the rift was really about as that would have sent the country into a flat spin. It all eventually ended when CDS decided to fall on his sword.

He walked out of the MOD and announced to the waiting press pack that due to a personal disagreement between the Prime Minister and himself he felt his position was untenable and for the good of the country he would step down. I watched the whole thing live on BBC news, telephoned him to offer my commiserations and then never saw him again he was reportedly killed in the Great Panic when the dead overwhelmed Salisbury.

The whole ruckus died down after that, the press lost interest and General Sir Richard Wolsey the former Chief of the General Staff, was appointed the new CDS over the objections of the PM. He really did not have any choice; he was the only one eligible for the position and the heads of the Navy and RAF felt that he was the best man to lead us through the coming storm.

With the press interest gone and the politicians blocking us at every turn we returned to the theoretical planning. British Operations are always identified by a code word and we eventually came up with Operation Senlac. The hill on which King Harold deployed his army for the Battle of Hastings against a foreign invader, appropriate no?

Authors note.

It was my intention at this point to interview a member of the Government at the time of the Great Panic, to provide a balanced view of the events detailed by Sir John Marsden.

Sadly, many the Cabinet had died in London in the early stages of the Great Panic and those survivors I approached declined to be interviewed.

Feral Youth

Manchester

Like most of the cities in post-war Britain, Manchester is a shadow of its former self. In the pre-war years, Manchester and the surrounding area was home to 2.5 million people and was considered the second city of England. The current population is around 20,000 all of whom live inside the Ring Road defensive wall. Gaz Taylor works on the City's Restoration and Recycling project the aim of which is to clear, demolish and recycle the city's vast suburbs with the intention of letting them return to nature. Gaz is currently working on a block of flats that was home to several hundred refugees during the Great Panic until an outbreak of Cholera killed them all.

I was unemployed at the beginning of the war; it was an easy time you know, no work, no jobs but steady benefit payments. Why would I bother my arse going to work when the Government paid me more money to do fuck all.

I had dropped out of school at 16 and had no idea what was going on outside my own bedroom window. All I could think about was doing something to keep myself busy and entertained and pretty soon I started to hang out with all the other unemployed kids. It was a pretty steady downward spiral from then on. Gangs, drugs, vandalising things, stealing anything we could get our hands on, that sort of shit.

The strange thing was I was pretty good at it. Within three years I had managed to move up the ranks. I was running my own patch and had started to spread into bigger and more profitable areas such as gun and drug smuggling and it was about this time that my crew started to get involved with the bigger organisations like the Triads, the Eastern European gangs and the Russians.

21

My crew specialised in getting small but high-value items into the city and passing them onto our contacts in the bigger international gangs. For a while it was easy street; not many cops are going to stop a 16-year-old kid on a bike with a backpack. Things started to get a bit more real once we were asked to start moving bigger and more sensitive stuff like organs and then pretty soon it became people.

Manchester had quite a large Chinese population with more and more arriving every year and unsurprisingly a huge trade in illegal workers and all the drugs, prostitution and gangs that come with it. We would act as the middlemen in the smuggling process, the snakeheads got them off the boats in Liverpool or at the airports and we moved them by car or truck into Manchester and then they disappeared into the city's underworld. It was fucking risky but the reward was worth it. I was the man of the patch, respected, feared. I could provide for my family and my Nan and I bought my first car at the age of 17 but at the time I didn't realise the damage I was doing.

What do you mean?

We brought the infection into the country.

Sure, it probably would have gotten here anyway; from 'fugees, infected business men, ferry travel and the Channel Tunnel, but without people like me the infected fugees from China and the illegal organs couldn't have gotten in and there wouldn't have been so many outbreaks all at once. People like me cause the Panic.

When did you realise things were going wrong?

We were starting to hear more and more stories from the fugees we were moving that things weren't right back home. There were two types back then, the rich and the poor. The poor came off the boats but were normally not a risk.

Why was that?

Journey time mate, it took weeks of travel by boat to get here or overland to the ports and even the slowest burn would have hit them way before they got anywhere near Britain. The problem was the rich ones. They came in by plane from Shanghai or Beijing, which in those days took a few hours, the ones who had a slow burn, you know a scratch or small bite, could last for days. We used to just meet them at the airport as cab drivers, drive them to a hotel, take the payment and leave them to it.

God knows how many infected organs were brought in by the Triads. The amount I moved in the months leading up to the Panic, well when you multiply that across the county then it is easy to understand why so many outbreaks happened in hospitals and back-alley clinics. Fuck, just look at that bloodbath in the Cromwell.

Did you ever see any infected?

I didn't know what I was looking for at the time. There was this one bloke though, a businessman travelling with his wife, he looked shit-scared and so did his misses. I had no idea what they were babbling about but I noticed a bandage around the husband's left arm. I dropped them at the hotel and went home. Next morning, I heard on the news that there had been a murder at the same hotel, a Chinese man had gone nuts, killed his wife and tried to eat her. He had attacked and bitten two police officers before he fell out the window in the struggle. It freaked me out I can tell you, I was certain that was the same guy I dropped off but couldn't think of a reason why he would have gone nuts. Didn't know then what I know now but it is easy to see that's how many of the outbreaks started. You know, infected fugees coming in and attacking people and those people going to the hospital and then reanimating. By the time I woke up and realised what was going on it was outside my house eating my fucking dog.

Other side of the Tracks

Henley-on-Thames, Oxfordshire

In the Pre-War years, Henley was the home of the renowned Henley Regatta, a summer rowing event that saw teams from across the world coming to compete. Despite the heavy clearance operations that took place on the Thames during the Restoration very little rowing takes place anymore. However, the first post-war regatta is due to take place this summer in a netted off and cleared section of the river. I am standing on the top deck of a houseboat with one of the event organisers, Charles Mulligan, as we watch the Militia on their third dive of the day. So far, they have brought up only three infected and there is hope that this dive will be uneventful and their last.

I used to live here before the war, did you know that. That house right over there by the riverside. It was my parent's house and when they died, it passed to me and my family. We lived there right up until the Great Panic before we ran like everyone else. I guess it kind of makes a poetic sense, I started The War here and then ended it here. It also makes me one of the lucky ones who actually managed to go home. So many people ended up scattered around the country and here I am back home, strange really.

What was your exposure to the virus before the Panic?

Very little if I am perfectly honest, I was just too busy. I used to work in the city for one of the big banks and had very little time for anything but that. I would wake up in the morning, get five minutes of news as I grabbed breakfast and then catch the train into work. I would read the paper on the way in but there was very little in there about any outbreaks, mostly it was to do with the awful state of the country and the world, how the economy was a mess and how we were all doomed generally. Life went on in my little commuter bubble.

So when was the first time that you realised that something was going on?

My wife worked as a volunteer nurse at the local health centre and began to hear some strange rumours circulating at work from the professional nurses. There were stories about people coming in with bites and then attacking hospital staff before being carted off by some military types, that sort of thing. We thought nothing of it at the time but then there was the "Rabies" outbreak in South Africa.

How did you hear about that?

Are you kidding? Every bloody news station was talking about it. There was nothing else on for days, just endless commentary, speculation and the footage from the South African police of the outbreak. All sorts of experts were on the TV commenting how the poor sanitation of the shanty towns and the social deprivation made a viral outbreak and social breakdown all but inevitable. So many people talking but no one was listening.

What was your reaction?

Probably the same as most people, I was scared shitless. The sheer amount of hype and utterly useless news coverage that did nothing but terrify people was absolutely unbelievable but I guess that is what happens in a 24-hour news cycle.

Everyone I knew was talking about the outbreak; was it going to be like SARS or Bird Flu or Swine Flu and not turn into anything major or was it the next Black Death? Would it make it over here? Was there a cure? I was concerned about how I would protect my family from infection and keep them safe if there was an outbreak over here. But then the anti-rabies drugs hit the market and everyone suddenly relaxed. I know now that we were sold a huge lie and that it was utterly useless but at the time it was the silver bullet that everyone was looking for. I will never say that I agree with what the company did by marketing it without proper testing or the Government for pushing it through NICE but I can understand. The country needed something to rely on and the Government needed to be seen to be taking action. I suppose if you were playing devil's advocate you could argue that the placebo put off the Great Panic for a year but then again, the ignorance of what we really faced was probably what killed so many people.

I take it you were on anti-virals?

Christ, I put everyone on the stuff. My wife, my kids, my parents, Olivia's parents, I even made the cleaner take it. I didn't want anyone around me who could possibly be infected. Looking back at it now, I am embarrassed about how I overreacted. I was well and truly part of the consumer machine ready to believe what the adverts told me and what the Government told me. It was how we all were back then.

When did things change for you?

Well in the first year it was all news hype and speculation, everyone on drugs, but then came winter. The reports of outbreaks from around the world dropped off and everyone relaxed a bit and let their guard down thinking it was over. It helped that the news channels got bored and went back to reporting on the celebrity gossip and the latest reality TV program.

It was when Israel announced its self-imposed quarantine that I sat up and took notice. I thought that if a country as paranoid and protective as Israel was taking this seriously then shouldn't we all be. That's when I started to think about how best to protect my family if the worst happened.

Oh, Bugger!

Charles points to the diver's safety line which is stretched taut and thrashing against the side. The line suddenly goes slack and is pulled in by the deck hands,

torn halfway along its length. There is no sign of the diver.

Senlac

Edinburgh Castle, Scotland

The Royal Military Headquarters is due to move to London in the next week. During the early days of the war, Edinburgh Castle was home to several thousand refugees before it was recaptured during the first phase of the Restoration and utilised as the HQ for the military as it pushed south. The HQ staff are in the process of packing up and moving to the new Ministry of Defence. The old MOD building on Whitehall burnt down during the Great Panic. The new MOD has been moved into the fully refurbished Horse Guards. I am interviewing the Chief of the Defence Staff, General Sir George Palmerston in his office in the former Governor's Wing of the Castle. General Palmerston has been CDS for the last two years following the death of General Sir Richard Wolsey. During The War, he served as the Vice Chief of the Defence Staff and was a party to every major decision.

Following the fracas outside the MOD when Air Chief Marshal Benford resigned and General Wolsey took over we decided that a change of approach was needed. There was no way that we would win in a stand-up fight, politically that is, with the Government. Their spin doctors would destroy us and they had the constitutional imperative. What I mean by that is we in uniform were beholden by our oaths of allegiance to the Monarch to follow the orders of "those Members of Parliament placed in positions of power under her". What this all meant was that we could not openly deny or disobey the Government. We had to be subtle, which was not something the military was ever particularly good at.

How did you get around the Government?

The simple answer is that we didn't. We decided to follow one of the oldest rules in the soldier's manual. BBB, Bullshit

Baffles Brains. We essential conceded to the Government on all their demands and promised not to mention in public the possibility of a "Zombie Plague". We showed with one hand that it was business as usual in the military but at the same time we kept on planning and war gaming and devising contingency plans with the other. When the time came we were as theoretically ready as it was possible to be.

Theoretically?

It had to be. Any effective military action intended to contain the threat would require putting troops on the streets and this would violate any number of laws unless approved by Parliament. As we were obviously not going to get it, we were limited to theoretical planning only.

Was that Operation Senlac?

It was still Exercise Senlac at that point and was actually a beautiful bit of staff work. It was also an incredibly appropriate name. Senlac was the hill on which King Harold fought the Battle of Hastings to defend his country from a foreign invader, rather appropriate don't you think.

The genesis of the plan was concocted by a very bored Captain during his work time. As I understand it he enjoyed the odd apocalypse film and novel and essentially wrote a plan for how to contain a national flu pandemic. The first time I saw it was when my Aide De Camp (ADC) handed it to me. Apparently, they were in the same platoon at Sandhurst and when outbreaks around the world started to be reported the officer sent it to my ADC with the tag line "Hope this can help".

Was it helpful?

Very, it formed the basis of the entire plan.

Can you give me a layman's version of Senlac?

Of course. The plan had six main phases; Containment, create Safe Zones, secure the Safe Zones, reorganise the population and the resources, retrain the Army and then retake the country. The first phase was intended to prevent a full-scale outbreak ever taking place by using Special Forces and specialist medical teams to contain and if necessary eliminate the infected. The remaining phases were a "just in case" it ever became an uncontrollable epidemic.

Eliminate?

A sad necessity really. It had become apparent very early on that there was no hope for someone once infected. All the Sanitation Teams could do was to contain and study those who were infected but not turned and eliminate those who had.

Evidently, the containment phase failed.

Sadly, yes and entirely due to political apathy. The problem we had was that the only way the containment phase would work was for people to be aware of the threat. By this, I mean the public and emergency services fully understanding what they were dealing with and being able to report and contain it so that the Sanitation Teams could go in and do their job. Look how much simpler it is today; everyone understands the threat and knows how to deal with it. It's why we allow the Militias to deal with the minor incidents and not send in the Army every time.

Of course, this sort of widespread education never took place. The Government was terrified of the panic such an announcement would cause. That is why so many of the initial outbreaks were such messy affairs and took so long for us to respond to. Our teams had to sit around and wait for outbreaks rather than being able to attack at the source.

So you went ahead without Government approval?

Damn right, you don't stand by and watch your house burn and not try to save it. Of course, we acted, the Government certainly wasn't going to but as I said the containment was a messy and patchwork affair and ultimately failed.

The next step was to create Safe Zones and this was relatively easy to do without Government approval. The MOD owned huge areas of land across the country as either training areas or bases and we had full and unrestricted access and control of that land. The first draft of the plan called for a Safe Zone to be established in Scotland and a physical barrier constructed to control the movement of the population. We developed this idea further by adding a second Safe Zone in Cornwall and then instigating the Burghs plan.

Burghs?

One of the officers working on the plan was a keen student of history and told us about the policy of Alfred the Great when facing the Viking invasions. He adopted a plan of defence in depth by building a wall around every town so that the marauding Vikings had nowhere to capture and use as a base. It also meant that the defenders could sally out and attack the raiders from a position of strength. Obviously, we could not build a wall around every city and town in the UK but what we did do was identify those locations that could be easily defended or reinforced and what units would capture and hold them.

Sadly, there were more sites than we had first thought and we soon realised that a degree of triage was necessary to ensure that we were not over-stretched. It meant abandoning many towns, villages and military camps but by the end of the process, we had identified some 200 locations throughout the country that could be defended almost indefinitely. We wrote the orders that would start the troops moving, give them their tasks and then sealed them waiting for the day we hoped would never come, but all secretly knew was inevitable. We also began to stockpile supplies, machinery and equipment behind the proposed Safe Zone lines.

Did the Government not catch on that something was up?

Why would they? At this point we had done nothing untoward, it was a theoretical paper exercise and we were fully with our rights to move our equipment and people wherever we liked.

What about the rest of the plan?

Well, the remaining three phases, the reorganisation, retraining and recapture were all planned in outline but all the detail would have to wait until after the other phases had happened. It was all dependent on the situation on the ground you see.

When did the plan go into effect?

Technically it was in effect as soon as CDS' signature was on the orders. However, it only really went live once those letters were opened by the Commanding Officers who had to carry out the orders and that only happened once the Panic really started. The Sanitation Teams were another matter though we had them operating right from the very beginning and after the first outbreak in South Africa we were operating with Government consent, at least for phase one, we were still prohibited from anything else.

Sorry, to answer your question. Op Senlac went live the morning after Cromwell Hospital.

First Responder

Rock, Cornwall

Constable Laura James is the village "Bobby" for this town. A life long police officer, she was part of the Police Armed Response team at the first major outbreak in London. We are currently walking the beat along the Rock coastal defences.

Built during The War to protect the town from sea incursions by Zombies they are now a tourist attraction and a number of shops and stalls have sprung up on the coastline to cater to the increase in visitors. Pre-War, swimming and surfing were major activities for the town but no one is willing to risk it today. While Royal Navy clearance operations of the English Channel are ongoing and productive, the coast of Britain still comes under regular attack, as evidenced by the rifle slung over Laura's shoulder and the mace hanging from her belt.

I had always wanted to be a Police Officer, ever since I was a little girl. An odd dream for a girl I know but there you go. I was never a doll and tea party kid and whenever the local children played Cops and Robbers I was always the Cop.

I grew up in London and joined the Metropolitan Police as soon as I left school. The training at Hendon Police College was hard but great fun and it was great to work and train with people who felt the same as me and had the same mindset. All those horror stories about bullying, racism and sexual discrimination, well I'm not saying it never happened but it never happened to me. I just got stuck in and did the best I could and never asked for any special treatment. I passed with good grades and got posted to a central London borough for my first two years. I wouldn't want to call the place a shit hole but let's just say that some areas of London were improved by the Great Fire. There was youth crime, drugs, ethnic issues, you name it the place had it. I learnt more in those two years than I ever thought possible.

Once my two years were up I decided to give the Armed Response teams a go. It took a lot of determination to sit through all the crap from senior officers about how it was not the best place for a woman and was I sure. Eventually, I got the green light and headed to Gravesend for the training and again loved every second of it; the marksmanship, advanced driving, abseiling off buildings, it was a tomboy's wet dream. I passed and was assigned to the Armed Response Vehicle teams. A team of three officers in a souped-up car would patrol an area and respond to any firearms incident as a rapid response unit. I did that for three years before the war.

When did you first encounter the Infected?

It was in the autumn of the first year about six months before everyone jumped on the panic wagon. We were on patrol in Hackney and there had been a number of gun-related incidents in the area, which at the time was put down to inter-gang violence. It was three in the morning and we got a call over the net that residents were reporting shots fired in the Argyle Estate and it was getting worse.

We hit the blue lights and shot off, getting there in about five minutes. When we arrived we were met by a terrified resident who told us that she had heard shots being fired somewhere on the fifteenth floor and a lot of shouting and screaming.

We took the emergency stairs up and came out at the end of the main corridor. The block was laid out along a central corridor with six flats on each side. We could see at the far end bullet holes pockmarking the walls and doors smashed in on three of the flats but the top two-thirds were untouched. About halfway along the corridor, an Asian man was slamming his fists into one of the doors. One of the team, Dave I think, yelled out "Armed Police. Get down on the ground and hands behind your head." The man turned our way, raised his arms as if he would grab us and then began lurching along the corridor towards us. It was only then that we could see the vacant look in his eyes and the blood covering his mouth and chest.

By this point, we were all a little bit freaked out but we thought the guy must be on drugs and had gone nuts. We couldn't shoot him as he wasn't armed but we still had to try and arrest him. Dave again warned the guy to get down or he would be Tasered. The guy didn't stop but just kept coming and moaning, Mike had already got his Tazer gun out and got the nod from Dave. He lined up the shot and fired. He went down and started twitching frantically as the volts randomly fired off all the nerve endings. Mike let off the trigger and just as we were about to take a step forward to arrest him, the guy sat up and started to get back on his feet. Now, there is no fucking way that even on drugs you are going to get up after that many volts have been pumped into you. We hit him again and again till the charge ran out of the gun and still nothing. We were properly bricking it now and knew we had to try and get the cuffs on this guy before he attacked us.

Mike was going to tackle him, Dave would pin his arms and I would get the cuffs on. We were about to launch ourselves at the junkie when there was this flash of light and a terrific bang. I remember reeling back dazed and blinded and then being smashed to the floor, I thought for a terrifying moment that the junkie had jumped me. But then I felt hands grabbing my arms and plasti-cuffs round my wrists, I shouted that I was police before a bag was put over my head. I could hear the soft "thwup" noise of silenced weapons and the thump of a body hitting the floor. I remember thinking that whoever these people were, they had just shot a civilian in cold blood.

It didn't end there. I counted about ten to fifteen shots being fired and then silence. I don't know how long it was before the regular Bobbies turned up and cut us lose but it couldn't have been more than ten minutes. What we found was twelve bodies; all shot in the head but there was no sign of

35

the guy who attacked us in the corridor. Some of the corpses had bite marks and chunks of flesh missing and there was blood all over the walls in three of the flats that had been broken into. The place looked like a slaughter yard, the kind of gore that horror movie directors can only dream about.

In one flat we found the remains of several Chinese people and bloody footprints leading to the flat opposite and then the bodies of two black youths, both armed and both torn to pieces. It was evident from the ballistics that they had been shooting at the attacker as he came through the door but not hit him before being torn apart. The final flat was a family of four, again all dead in their bedroom, it was evident from the way they were lying that they had tried to take shelter in a corner before being killed.

The initial investigation put it down to a new form of drug that turned people into frothing madmen but made no mention of who had attacked us. It was all very suspicious but I was more concerned with surviving the interviews and salvaging my career.

What do you think happened?

Well, it is obvious now that it was an outbreak that was contained by one of the Sanitation Teams.

Did you know of any other incidents like yours?

Once I knew what I was looking for I started to collate reports of other incidents with similar characteristics. It became evident that there had been a number of "drug-related" attacks in major cities all over the country, mainly focused on areas with a high Chinese population or in hospitals. I took my findings to my Chief who said she would look into it and get back to me. About a week later the first outbreaks happened and I assumed we were dealing with a Rabies outbreak and not a new drug. Then the anti-virals hit the markets, winter came and I noticed a marked drop in cases, until the next spring.

Can you tell me about the Cromwell Hospital?

(**Shivers**) What a fucking mess. It was about a month after the Israelis announced their quarantine. I was off duty in a Police Station near Kensington when the call came through of an outbreak in the Cromwell Hospital. By this time, we thought we knew what we were dealing with and had developed tactics to deal with it.

Can you explain those assumptions and tactics?

Well, like everyone else we thought that we were dealing with a rabies virus that turned the infected into a berserker like assailant who would attack and try to eat anyone they came across. They could be shot but would not feel it and only a headshot would take them down straight away. We had been given special rules of engagement that told us that we should try to "subdue and arrest" the attackers and only if we were in mortal danger could we shoot. So fucking stupid given what we know now.

Anyway, we got the call that there had been an outbreak in the surgical wing of the Cromwell and we needed to respond. The initial brief was that a single man had attacked a surgical team during his operation and killed them all before breaking out of the ward and attacking random patients. There were an estimated 50 dead or wounded and the hospital was being evacuated.

We got there just as the news teams did. There were streams of patients and staff leaving the hospital some of whom I am certain had been bitten. Looking back, it is easy to see how Cromwell kicked off the whole meltdown in London. One attacker bites but doesn't kill a number of people, they all flee the hospital, start getting ill and are rushed to nearby hospitals only to die, reanimate and then start the whole cycle again. I am sure similar things must have happened in other cities as well.

Anyway; we arrived, got a briefing from the on-site commander and moved into the building in teams of four. Our orders were to sweep the building from the ground floor to the roof and arrest any attackers within. Medical staff would follow behind us and patch up the wounded.

We moved in through the lobby, past patients and staff still evacuating and headed toward the surgical wing and the recovery wards. The security staff had managed to seal the doors with a heavy metal bar and through the window, we could see no movement. My team and another pulled aside the bar and as quietly as possible moved into the ward. I tell you what, when Dante wrote his Inferno he was underestimating what hell was like. The place was an abattoir, no worse than that, abattoirs are at least organised and sanitary, this looked like someone had gone mad with a chainsaw.

There was blood splatter all over the walls and in pools on the floor, body parts were strewn everywhere. There were some patients who had obviously been unconscious from the surgery and drugs when they were attacked as they were still lying in their beds in hospital gowns. They looked as if they had been eaten while they were asleep. Hell of a way to go, although probably better than being awake. We passed maybe twenty to thirty corpses but still no sign of the attacker.

We were about two-thirds of the way through the ward when we began to hear this banging from up ahead. We moved forward as a group, all eight of us as tense and alert as humanly possible. I don't think I have ever been that scared in all my life, my heart was going like a freight train; we were all sweating and shaking from the adrenaline. We turned a corner and three meters away, found our attacker. He was probably in his late fifties, very overweight, and was wearing a surgical gown that was open at the back giving us a perfect view of a flabby arse and surgical stitches by his right kidney. He was banging away on an office door, from behind which we could hear screams and whimpering. We took up a firing line and then as per the rules yelled at him to get down on the ground. His head spun around and I found myself having a flashback to that council block corridor.

The man turned and lurched towards us, arms raised and moaning. We yelled again for him to stop and then before we could act he was on one of the guys from the other team. He grabbed his arms and within a heartbeat had bitten down into the guy's neck. He screamed as blood spurted over the attacker but we were all frozen in terror. I snapped out of it first and slammed the butt of my sub-machine gun on the attacker's head. It looked like he was stunned for a second before he turned, looked straight at me and then lunged, blood pouring from his open mouth. I screamed and shot him point blank in the face before I collapsed to the floor sobbing hysterically.

I am not afraid to say I was fucking terrified at the time. The guys were busy trying to save their teammate from bleeding out and my team were going forward to help the people in the office. I pulled myself together and started to see where I could help. I moved toward the office and found three terrified nurses and a doctor who were slowly being coaxed out from behind a desk. I looked at my team leader and suggested we get these people and our casualty out. I could see the fear in his eyes as he agreed with me and we started to move back towards the ward entrance. That was when it all went Pete Tong.

We had just gotten back into the main post-op ward when one of the nurses screamed and pointed at one of the beds. One of the half-eaten corpses had sat up and was looking straight at us. Its arms came up and it moaned before lurching off the bed and slouching towards us. I looked around and started to see other corpses moving; bodies that we had stepped over or checked for signs of life were getting up and moving towards us. I took a quick look around and realised we were about to be surrounded. The senior officer from the other team yelled "back to back" and we formed a tight circle with the casualty, the doctor and the nurses at the centre. One of the nurses was behind me and was clinging to my harness, whimpering "Oh God, Oh God" over and over right in my ear.

I think everyone was frozen, no one moved, no one acted. I could hear the frantic conversation between the team, things like. "What do we do?"

"I don't know!"

"We've got to do something; we can't stay here!"

"Shoot the fuckers."

"We can't, rules of engagement."

I think at that point someone said, "Fuck that!" and opened fire. That was it, we all just let rip, no aimed shots, no head shots just panicked firing from the hip into the crowd. I must have gone through two magazines before I realised nothing was happening, we were hitting them, they were being knocked back but then, terrifyingly they were getting up and coming straight back at us.

How did you get out?

We broke, simple as that. The nurse behind me couldn't take it and had been screaming in my ear the entire time. She pushed her way past me and made a break for the door ten meters away. She made it maybe three meters before a man pulling himself along the floor, half-eaten legs dragging behind him caught her foot and brought her crashing down. Three other attackers were on her before she could move, grabbing, biting and tearing. It gave us a gap in the line and we all ran for it.

Some made it, others didn't. I was one of the last and leapt over a scrum of attackers who had one of my team on the floor. I was caught by the ankle in mid-air and came down hard on my face on the other side next to the door. I rolled onto my back and saw one of them coming for me, crawling along the floor. It grabbed my foot and tried to pull itself up my body. I screamed and pulled the trigger, blowing off the top of its head. I frantically started to backpedal along the floor trying to get to my feet but too panicked to coordinate the effort.

I eventually crawled to my feet and ran for the entrance, through the doors and into the artificial sunlight of God knows how many camera lights. I staggered in the dazzling light before I was knocked to the ground and a man in a black combat suit and balaclava pointed a gun at me. "Are you bitten, any open wounds?" he yelled at me. I shook my head before being tied up and led to a waiting ambulance to be checked over.

At the same time, twenty similarly dressed men were preparing to enter the hospital when the doors slammed open and a horde of the attackers poured out into the car park. The cameras caught the whole thing, the attackers lurching down the steps and then being cut down by the men in black, the screams of the civilians and the shocked but gleeful shouts of the press. I remember hearing the paramedic checking me muttering "My God it is all true!" I asked what he meant but he just shook his head. I found out later that a reporter in America had gone public about five minutes before with the truth. You know, that it wasn't a new strain of rabies after all, that it was actually a virus that reanimated the dead and turned them into rampaging killers and that the anti-virals did fuck all to stop it.

It was perfect timing; you know like the Devil having a laugh. The raw truth followed by a healthy dose of hospital massacre based evidence plastered all over the 24-hour news channels. It's no wonder that country flipped, no one can take that much truth in one go. I certainly couldn't, by the time I got a clean bill of health the world had gone to hell in a handcart and I was running for Cornwall as fast as I could.

PANIC

CCTV operator

Alnwick, Northumberland

Tarik Kahn is not the cliché image of an English Country Farmer. Since the Consolidation, he has been a tenant on the Duke of Northumberland's Estates around Alnwick Castle, the historical seat of the Percy family for 700 years. During the Great Panic, the Duke of Northumberland offered sanctuary to several hundred refugees in the castle. During the Consolidation, these refugees took part in the clearance of the surrounding area and were offered land to farm and hold in a modern form of tenant farming. Tarik was one of those offered the land that he still farms with his family today. Before The war, Tarik was a CCTV operator for the London Metropolitan Police based in the Police Emergency Control Centre in Lambeth.

It was often said that the British were the most watched society in the world; the simple fact is that most newspapers and civil liberties groups would have been shocked at the things we could see and hear. Lambeth was home to the Emergency Command Centre for the Met and from there we could access any of the CCTV cameras in the entire London area as well as any number of cameras from cash points, shops or banks; we could even get the feed from unprotected home CCTV systems. It was not all strictly legal but it was incredibly effective when you were looking for a suspect.

Lambeth was also an incredible building. The entire place was built to survive a terrorist attack on London; it had food supplies, water recycling, its own generators and the entire building could be sealed to prevent a physical attack. The only thing the designers had not planned for was a flood. The building was close to the Thames and if it had burst its banks then the whole command centre would have been underwater.

I understand that you were there during the Great Panic.

Yes, I was. Most people think that the Great Panic was an instantaneous freakout like everyone just went nuts at once. It just wasn't like that at all; the whole thing actually started very slowly and then just built up momentum. The Cromwell was the loose pebble that started the whole rock slide.

I was on duty that day and we had front row seats to the entire thing. We had good coverage from the cameras outside but we also had access to the security feeds from inside the building and we saw the whole thing. We watched the first infected killing his own surgical team then breaking out and killing all the people in the surgical ward, the police coming in and getting surrounded and then the final clearance by the Sanitation Teams. I never found out who did it but I know for a fact that someone in my team leaked the recordings to the media. Talk about pouring petrol on a fire.

Can you tell me how the Panic started?

Well as I said it all started quite slowly. Initially, it was people packing up and trying to get out of London, there was the odd outbreak at a hospital that the police and military tried to contain but then it just got faster and faster you know; riots, fires, people looting, all that stretched the police more than the infected. The Government was trying to keep control and maintain an air of normalcy by using the police but it was like trying to bail a sinking ship with a thimble.

It took three days for the country to just go mad. The roads started to get filled up with cars packed to the roof with useless stuff. It looked like something I saw in a documentary on the Indian railways, you know, people hanging off trains, sitting on top of cars that sort of thing.

Even on a good day, London was a congested nightmare and those first few days were definitely not good. It took about five minutes of half the city trying to get on the roads for the whole place to become gridlocked. People would get frustrated, angry and scared, fights would break out, people would get killed and then there would be one more roadblock in the way. We could see people trying to fight the infected, trying to run from them, people settling old scores with rivals, the infected weren't the only thing killing people in those first few days. We saw the swarm in Trafalgar Square come pouring down the Mall and attacking the Guards. God knows how many civilians those brave bastards saved.

Then there were the dead; pouring out of the hospitals, the council estates and houses, we could actually see the swarms multiplying as they killed or infected people and they then reanimated to infect again. The infection just spread faster and faster and it seemed no one was doing anything to stop it.

On top of it, all was the fact that the media was broadcasting the whole thing; the stupid bastards were spreading panic around the country and fanning the flames. Most of the major cities panicked the same time as London and the rest of the country went right along with it.

How did you escape?

I was one of the fortunate ones in the surveillance team. I was single, my parents and family all lived in Bradford. One of the first things I did was to call them and tell them to get out and find somewhere to hide. Unfortunately, they didn't take it seriously and I never heard from them again. We spent the first week of the Panic holed up in the Control Room trying to coordinate the police and fire response. After the second week, we realised it was a pretty wasted effort and then in the third week The Fire started.

Did you see it begin?

Honestly no. There were so many small fires across the city that I don't think there was only one cause. The fire brigade was so stretched just trying to contain them and protecting themselves from looters, panicked people and infected that they just couldn't cope. I know that the fires seemed to gain real strength in Elephant and Castle and just spread east.

Did you know the reason why all the old industrial areas of the city are in the east? It is because the wind normally blows from the west and would have kept all the industrial smoke and soot away from the posh areas. That wind was now pushing and combining the fires and they just marched across the city and burnt everything in its path. The rest of the city was burning in isolated pockets that would spread outward from a single point and just keep going until it ran out of fuel.

I met a guy in Glasgow who had worked on the European satellite network and he told me it was like watching ink falling on blotting paper. I read in the Olsen Report that something like 90% of the city burnt down, God knows how much crap that threw into the air but it's no wonder that first winter was so harsh.

Anyway, the higher-ups decided to evacuate us to the back-up command location in Hendon and I stayed there until just before the Battle of Junction. After that, we just made a break for it and tried to make it to the Safe Zone in Scotland. We got halfway there on a police helicopter before it ran out of fuel near Hull, then we walked the rest of the way. We made it as far as Alnwick before we realised we couldn't go on any further. Of the twenty of us who started only six were left and even then, we were in terrible shape. I had a broken leg and a fever, we were all malnourished and exhausted. The Duke took us in, looked after us, fed us and I have been here ever since. I guess I had it easy compared to some of the poor bastards out there.

The Battle of The Mall

Port Stanley, Falkland Islands

The Falkland Islands suffered heavily during The War but not from the infected themselves. Following the collapse of the Argentinean Government and the fall of Buenos Aires the vast majority of the population fled to the Andes in search of sanctuary. However, a significant portion made for the Falkland Islands in the hope of security. The Islands fell to the Argentine refugees and Britain was in no position to intervene. Two years after Victory in Britain Day (VB Day), Britain sent an amphibious task force to recapture the Islands and reclaim the oil fields beneath. Part of the task force was Company Sergeant Major James "Jock" MacTavish, Scots Guards who has since retired and settled in Stanley as part of the Island Self Defence Force. He joined the Army a year before The War and served with distinction in all of his regiment's operations, his first battle was The Mall.

Talk about bad timing, I had joined the Army the summer before the first outbreak and had gone straight to Phase 1 training in Catterick. Six months later and seventeen years old I was sized up for a tunic and bearskin and tramping around London on public duties with F Company Scots Guards. At the time, all new recruits would go through London for a year before joining their Battalions. Get a feel for the ceremonial, regimental history thing you know.

I arrived just as things were beginning to get twitchy and we were starting to get briefed up on the threat. Most of us thought it was a joke the first time we got the briefing but fairly soon we started to see all the preparation work that was going on and thought "Hang on, there might be something to this!"

What sort of thing did they brief you on?

It was a pretty basic outline really. They gave us the low down of the enemy, their motivation, patterns that sort of thing. It was quite funny really, this Intelligence Officer standing there trying to give a proper military brief on the threat with all these conventional war terms like Enemy, Objective, Threat and all the while he was talking about something that should be in a movie. It went right over my head I tell you. My Platoon Commander summed it up for us; he said "Right lads, basic version. Don't let the bastards bite you or you die. Don't let anyone who has been bitten into camp because they will die, then you will die. If you want to kill them; shoot them in the head and they will die. Simples!"

What type of preparations did you take?

Well for starters was the fact that we were all on 24 hours' notice to move, which is basically where you have all your kit packed ready to go. Apparently, the last time we did this was after 7/7.

What else?

There was the stockpiling of food and ammunition. I was part of a work party that was unloading ammunition from a delivery vehicle to one of the ammo bunkers. I swear to God there was enough there to invade France. There were other things as well; food, bedding, dogs and heavy engineer vehicles started to arrive in Wellington Barracks and that was shit we never saw in London. I remember speaking to the Quarter Master during the siege and asking him why we were so well provisioned. He told me that the Barracks Commanding Officer had received a warning order during the winter that ordered him to begin stockpiling supplies and preparing the barracks for a long siege.

Wait, you said that the barracks was prepared for a siege but didn't you end up in the Palace?

I'll get to that in order if that's OK?

Sure.

Ok so we were preparing for a siege and getting briefings about the enemy and all that and then the Cromwell happens, that reporter goes to press with the truth and we all get mobilised. We go from red tunics and empty rifles to combats and full warfighting scales of ammo. It was incredible; almost overnight the barracks was transformed into a fortress. All the gates were sealed and some of the more vulnerable ones were blocked with shipping containers, we built an infected clearing centre in the central car park out of cars and barbed wire. I don't know if you know Wellington Barracks but the side facing Birdcage Walk was massively vulnerable, only a ten-foot-high iron railing fence and then a big open parade square. We built a second wall made from containers right up against the fence and built fire positions on top.

By the third day of the panic we were as ready as we could be, we had a fucking fortress and we were ready to defend it. What we didn't count on was the hordes of civilians outside trying to get in.

How did you deal with it?

Well, the Commander's official policy was to not let anyone in but pretty soon we had all had more than we could stand. You have no idea how hard it is to sit inside your fortress and hear the world ending outside, knowing you can help but not being allowed to. It went on like this for a couple of days before there was almost a fucking mutiny and the Commander caved in and allowed us to start admitting people.

Surely there was a rush of people, how did you control it?

We parked a JCB right by the gate which stopped it being forced and then opened it enough to allow one person through at a time. We dragged them through and herded them into the clearing centre. We only let in about a hundred at a time and once they were all in we sent them past the dog cages one at a time. First time around we had no idea why but after the dogs went mental and we found our first infected we found out.

How did you deal with the infected?

(Jock looks down and slight quaver comes into his voice) We disposed of them?

Disposed?

Yeah.

Can you elaborate?

No. We did our job and we kept people alive. Can we move on, please?

Ok. How many refugees did you end up taking in?

By the end of the second week, we had close to a thousand and then we had to stop. We just didn't have space or supplies. Besides by that point, most people had left London and were on their way north. It was only us and the Gs.

Were there many by that point?

At first no, I guess most of them were chasing the refugees and as I heard later, eating their way up the motorways. They would turn up in ones and twos and we could normally deal with those. We had teams of lads scattered around the perimeter slotting the Gs as they appeared, trying to keep the numbers down. It was only when The Fire started that we started to see more.

How did The Fire affect you?

We got evicted.

The barracks was surrounded on three sides by high rise buildings and the fire was getting closer and closer. You could see it from the roof, thick columns of smoke rising into the sky and flattening out, casting the city into a weird perpetual twilight and all the Gs were being driven in front of it.

The Commander realised that the barracks would probably catch fire given the height of some of the buildings around us and he decided to move to Buckingham Palace. By this time we were properly under siege with probably a couple of thousand Gs around us.

The plan was that we would get all our supplies and ammunition and as many of the civis as possible onto the trucks, break out of the barracks and run for the south gate of the Palace. Nijmegen Company would block Buckingham Gate, 7 Coy would block Birdcage Walk, F Coy The Mall and the Buckingham Palace Guard would take Constitution Hill. At the same time, the Massed Bands would act as protection for the refugees as they crossed.

We had found out pretty early on that Gs were pretty basic and would go were the food was, so we hung over the wall on the Petty France side of the barracks and for two days yelled and shouted at the Gs to try and get as many of them on the other side of the camp as possible. We also shot as many of them as we could just to give ourselves a better chance when the time came.

When D-Day finally arrived, we were all bricking it. We were all in light scales so that we could run as fast as possible but with as much ammo as we could carry. The JCB went out first with its dozer blade lowered and cleared the first lot away from the gate, we all followed out slotting those that had been mangled by the dozer and trying to shoot as many of those nearby as possible. I know that a lot of armchair generals have said how difficult it was to transition from aiming for centre mass to headshots and it was at first but we had had two weeks of practice from inside the fence so we all felt pretty confident.

Anyway, we broke out and began to move to our set lines. We would leapfrog past one another forming a line as we went. In my case 7 Company went first their lead man going out the gate and then straight onto one knee and started firing, the next guy would run a meter past him and then go to ground. We repeated this till 7 Coy had Birdcage Walk blocked and then we kept going past them onto The Mall and set up our firing line. It was like something out of a Zulu movie. A single line of lads, shoulder to shoulder facing down the Mall; if we had been wearing our tunics it would have been perfect.

Initially, we thought that we had the easy job as The Mall was pretty much empty but then the first Gs started to appear through Admiralty Arch. We didn't know it at the time but we had chosen to break out just as one of the really big swarms had hit Trafalgar Square and they were being drawn straight towards us by the noise of the gunfire.

I could feel the lads either side of me shaking with either fear or adrenaline, I know that my own shakes were definitely based on fear. You don't kneel in the middle of a massive road and watch a horde of fucking zombies heading toward you and not feel scared. You could sense all the lads were shitting it and ready to run. We could hear all the gunfire behind us and the engines as the trucks rolled out. The Company Commander obviously sensed it as well; he stepped out of the line and stood right in front of us. He turned his back to the Gs and said in a very calm voice. "Right lads, we've got a bit of a scrap ahead of us." Typical bloody officer understatement!

"I want every man to keep calm, keep breathing and we will get through this together. Aim for the head and keep the shots slow and steady. No one fires until I give the word."

He then turned to the Company Sergeant Major and told him to "Carry on, I going to get my eye in". The Company Commander then turned away and as if he was on a fucking game shoot just started picking off the leading Gs in the oncoming horde. The Company Sergeant Major "carried on" by yelling that the first person to shoot without orders, he would "shove his pace stick up his arse and ride him around the Buckingham Palace forecourt like a fucking Stick Pony." We all burst out laughing and felt the nerves fall away.

By then the Commander was falling back into line and raised his hand, the horde was three hundred meters away. "On my order, Fire!" we let rip with a ragged volley and the Gs at the head of the horde shuddered and collapsed. Two seconds had passed.

"Take aim, Fire!" another two seconds and we fired again. We went on like this for longer than I can remember but the horde just got closer and closer. At one hundred meters we were told to fire at will and the noise became a rolling wall of thunder.

"Right lads, we're doing well. Civis are almost across and we can start moving back."

I can tell you that when a horde of Gs are only a hundred meters away and the civis are only half across things are definitely not moving fast enough for my liking. The Company Commander decided that the Gs were close enough and he sent half the Company another hundred meters down The Mall to form a second line. The Gs were now only fifty meters away and the Company Commander gave the word for us to fall back. We broke to either side of the road and ran like bastards, while the guys in the second line kept firing straight down the middle. I tell you what I probably gave Usain Bolt a run for his money that day.

We did probably two more leaps before we found ourselves on the steps of the Queen Victoria memorial and flanked by the other Companies who had also been pushed back. I remember taking a quick glance around and seeing a shuffling horde of Gs closing in from all sides. We were knocking them down but there were just so many of them. That was when the shooting started to get ragged as some of the lads started flapping and hurrying their shots. The Gs got closer and we stepped further back. The Company Commander was right behind me and I could hear over his headset that they were considering just legging it for the gate. A few seconds later the order came over the radio; rear rank would break off first and line the inside of the Palace fence and start firing outwards, then the rest would follow.

As soon as the order came I legged it for the gate and once in took up a place by the fence. I can't tell you how good it felt to have a physical barrier between the Gs and me.

Once those on the inside began firing the rest broke off and ran. They all made it inside and the only hairy moment was when we closed that gate. Some of the lads had cut it a bit fine and were slipping through the gate with Gs right on their arse and the gate was in danger of being forced by the sheer weight of them trying to get through. Thank God the QM saw the danger and drove the digger right up against it and closed the gate. I think at that point we all just stood around breathing heavily and trying to get the adrenalin out of our systems. Of course, no one is allowed to stand around for long in the Army and pretty soon the Sergeant Major was yelling at us to form up in Companies for a roll call. It was only then that I noticed how badly mauled Nijmegen and 7 Company were, they looked like they had lost half of their lads in the fight.

How long were you in the Palace for?

Actually, not that long. We had timed the move pretty well and there was an evacuation planned for the next day to get the last of the Royal Family out to one of the Safe Zones. We managed to get on the radio and advise the HQ of the situation and they promised to send help to evacuate us. It turned up in the form of four Chinook helicopters. What we weren't told was that it was only the military and the Royals who were being pulled out. The civis and palace staff cottoned on pretty fast and there was almost a fucking riot. It was only stopped when we fired over their heads.

It was the hardest thing I have ever had to do, being told to leave those people that we had fought for, some of us had died for, to their fate. I was one of the last to get on the heli and I remember looking at this one guy, he was the de-facto leader of the civis and had managed to hold them back. I caught his eye and said something lame like "We'll come back for you." He smiled and replied, "I'll hold you to that."

I kept my word though. Took a while but I was there, the first man through the gate when we liberated the Palace. He was still there; still, the leader and he had just been named the official Governor of Buckingham Palace by the King. Nice to have a happy ending because I was not feeling that way as the Chinooks took off. As we flew over the city we got a birds-eye view of The Fire and the devastation before we headed North.

Where did you end up?

I went home to Scotland and rejoined my Regiment.

Safety at Sea

Caernarfon, Wales

Dan Brightman has been a resident of Caernarfon since the Great Panic and is now a member of the Castle Council, responsible for security in the local area. This is the first year that no infected have been seen in the local area, although there is the odd incursion from the sea.

I started the Panic in my student digs at Liverpool University. I was in my second term as a Fresher, having a great time and had just had an amazing holiday in Val d'Isere with my mates. I was definitely not focused on some zombie rumour that was floating around campus.

Did people not talk about it at Uni?

Not really at first but when more and more information began to appear on the internet it started to get mentioned. People would pass around stories and clips from YouTube, I got sent a load of things from outbreaks in South Africa, India, China all over the world really. That's when it all got a bit more real for me you know. I spoke to my parents about once a month and I would try and make them understand that this was probably something they should take seriously but they were normal middle-class people you know and were confident that the Government would take care of it. I think like the rest of the country they were just not ready to believe something so unbelievable.

What happened to you during the Panic?

It was about a week after the Cromwell and some friends and I were in my room in halls. We were watching the news and scouring the internet trying to find out what was going on. I had called my parents that morning and found out they were getting out of London and heading north to try and get to Scotland, they made me promise I would stay safe and try and meet up with them. They had heard on the news that the infected freeze in the cold and so naturally thought to head north, neither of them were the outdoors type though. Dad was a banker and Mum a housewife, I think the closest they have ever been to camping is at Garsington or Henley. It just goes to show how ill-prepared our "modern" society was and how much they panicked.

What do you mean?

Come on, you just have to look at the lifestyle of most of the population of the country back then. Unhealthy diets, very little exercise, no knowledge of life outdoors or even basic survival skills and I'm sorry but watching Bear Grylls or Ray Mears does not count.

Most people had never been outside their quiet, urban lives. Was it any wonder that so many people died in that first winter; exposure, starvation, thirst, exhaustion and that's not to mention those killed by the infected. I think the Olsen Inquiry estimated that something like 30 million people died in the Panic and the "Zombie winter", that's just under half of the pre-War population.

Can you imagine some office worker who spends their entire life commuting to work or sat at their desk all day; walking from London to Scotland while fighting off the infected? It's no wonder half the corpses on the roads north weren't getting back up again. They had dropped dead because nothing in their daily lives had prepared them for the end of that form of life. We were soft and weak and when it came down to it good old Darwinian "survival of the fittest" swung in and made sure we got a bloody good kicking.

That's a bit of a cold outlook, isn't it?

I'm sorry, I don't mean to be harsh or rant but it just makes me so angry you know! We did this to ourselves, our own laziness and lifestyle brought about the Panic.

You don't blame the Government?

No, they did their best to control the situation but how do you control millions of people all acting irrationally. Have you ever noticed how when humans get together in large groups, some sort of herd instinct takes over, you can see it at football matches? Get enough people going and you end up with a massive riot on your hands and no clear reason why it started, everyone just joins in. How was the Government or the military going to control that?

No, I blame people for the Panic. I blame you, me, my parents; we are all equally responsible for what happened. Sorry I'm ranting I know, ask anyone at the local pub, this is a subject you don't want to get me started on.

Anyway, I had told my parents I was going to find somewhere safe to hole up and then try and meet up with them in Scotland. My friends and I had a plan to make a break for the port, find a boat and then head up the coast. We packed as much food and equipment as we could carry and headed out on to the streets. Big mistake!

How so?

We had all been so focused on the TV and internet, trying to find out what was going on around the country that none of us had bothered to look out the window. We didn't realise that Liverpool was going through the same chaos as London.

The student campus on Lime Street was quite quiet but as soon as we got into the city proper and headed toward the river we realised that everyone else had the same idea. There were thousands of people crammed onto the streets pushing and shoving. The crowd was like water, flowing and surging, carrying people with it. There were twenty of us in our little group and within seconds we had been split apart by the crowd. I managed to keep hold of three of my friends and we had no choice but to go with the flow, literally.

Half the city must have been out on the streets, no one really knowing what was happening, or what direction they were travelling in but just following everyone else in the vain hope that someone knew where safety was. It was just like how you thought the end of the world would be, cars turned over and on fire, shouting, screaming, bodies lying where they fell and almost like a background orchestra to the apocalypse was the constant moan of the infected. You could hear them everywhere and that was the worst part; it wasn't like they were coming from one direction and people were running the opposite way, they were everywhere, all around. Every few seconds there would be more screaming and shouting as a group of them attacked. The crowd would surge away and then another attack, pushing people in another direction. It must have looked like a shoal of fish being attacked by sharks, just flowing this way and that to avoid the predators. God, it was horrible.

Somehow the three of us managed to stay together, clinging to each other for dear life. Every now and then one of us would get separated by a sudden surge in the crowd and we would have to frantically try and grab at each other. It happened more times than I could count but after about ten minutes of this, we decided to strike out down the side streets to try and go around the crowd.

Another big mistake. Sure we were not going to get trampled by thousands of panicked people but we had to contend with the looters and the infected that would lunge out of every alley or doorway. We pretty much spent the whole time running and avoiding anything that moved. One of my friends, Lucy, was grabbed as we passed the Cavern Club. A hand shot out from behind some bins and grabbed her by the hair. She screamed and was yanked onto her back. We turned around and got to her just as the infected got its hands on her backpack. It was a tug of war with the infected pulling one way and us the other. We were so panicked that we didn't think to undo the straps, eventually, they snapped and we fell backwards in a heap with the zombie going the other way, still clutching the backpack. It tossed it aside and started coming for us, I tell you I have never moved so fucking fast in my whole life. We were up and running before the thing had taken two steps.

I can't remember much of the next few minutes but we ran for our lives. Every now and then I get nightmares of that run, flashbacks that come back to haunt me. Fucking terrible.

We eventually burst out onto the docks expecting to see boats and ships, hell anything that floated. Instead, we got bugger all, just more people. We hadn't realised, being students and having lived in Liverpool for all of three months that all the proper docks were in the north of the city and we had come out by Albert Docks, the renovated tourist area near the city centre. Evidently loads of other people had the same idea as there must have been a thousand people milling around.

I grabbed my friends and began pushing my way to the quayside by the river thinking to try and hail a boat passing by. We made it to the edge and looked out across the Mersey to see hundreds of boats, barges, ships and tenders. You name it, if it floated, it was on the river. We waved and screamed for them to come and get us but they just kept on going right by. All of sudden we heard screams behind us and felt the crowd surge our way. I overbalanced and went head first into the river. I came up floundering and looked up just as someone crashed down on top of me. I was forced deeper into the water and frantically fought my way to the surface. I looked around and saw that I had been pushed upstream from the quay and further into the river. I looked back and could see people jumping or being forced off the quay as a pack of infected ate their way through the crowd. I couldn't see my friends.

By now things were getting pretty crowded and I struck out for the passing ships. I considered myself quite a strong swimmer but I was knackered by the time I had gone a hundred meters. I started to find it harder and harder to keep myself above water and I remember thinking that at least if I drowned I wouldn't reanimate. I was just about to go under when I felt something grabbing my backpack; I thought an infected must have grabbed me and started to thrash around trying to fight it off. It was only when this scouse accent yelled in my ear "Stop fighting you wanker I'm trying to save your life" that I relaxed.

I found myself on the deck of a garbage barge with around fifty other people all in similar states of shock, some bloodied, bandaged and all wet. I remember sitting on a sack of rubbish with a mug of tea that someone had passed to me watching as a dying city slid past. It was one of the most surreal moments of my life; no one spoke, we just watched, numb, as Liverpool burned in front of us.

It was only when we entered the mouth of the estuary that someone piped up and asked what the plan was. No one seemed to have any ideas except that we needed to find somewhere safe to stop or we would all starve. Someone mentioned that they remembered something about a castle at Caernarvon in Wales and that it might be a good place to hide. After a bit of a debate, we agreed to follow the coastline until we found the castle or somewhere better to stay.

It took three days on a stinking barge in some of the worst weather on record, God it was bloody miserable but we made it eventually. We passed under the Menai Bridge that separates Anglesey from Wales as a horde of infected moaned and grabbed for us from both shores and fell from the bridge above us.

I remember seeing the castle from the river as we approached and thinking it was the most beautiful thing I had ever seen. There was no one in sight as we docked at the quay below the castle and made for the gate. We were stopped just before we got there by a shotgun blast into the air.

It turned out that the town council had managed to get a portion of the town into the castle before the outbreak got out of hand and had been happily held up with electricity and running water. They let us approach and once we got to the main gate they told us that they would only allow us in if we were inspected, naked. There was a lot of shouting at this but I could see the reason behind it; why let possibly infected people into your secure castle who could possibly reanimate and kill you.

I was the first to step forward. I was stripped naked and inspected for any bites, cuts or infected wounds, which thankfully I did not have and then allowed into the castle. After this everyone else submitted except for one or two people, they hung back and refused to be searched clutching arms or hands to their chests. It was obvious they had a slow burn and were terrified of being turned away but the castle guards were having none of it and kept them separated from the rest of us. It was the most heart-breaking thing I have ever seen; the portcullis closing with those people on the other side left to fend for themselves.

What happened to them?

They stayed outside the main gate for two days before one of them died. The others ran off before she could reanimate and we never saw them again. The woman reanimated and was shot by one of the locals who had a hunting rifle. We burnt her body the next day.

What happened to you after that?

Well, we integrated ourselves into castle life and I have been here ever since. It wasn't easy by any stretch of the imagination but it was a damn sight better than those poor bastards I left behind in Liverpool.

Senlac Phase 2

Junction 47, A1(M)

I have been asked to accompany General Palmerston as he begins his journey south to London. The General has chosen to drive so he can inspect the new, permanent motorway defensive walls that have taken over from the wartime fortifications. We have stopped at the war memorial commemorating the famous last stand of 2nd Battalion the Mercian Regiment to pay our respects.

The Panic was without a doubt one of the busiest few months of my life and from a purely academic point of view, it was amazing how wrong we were on our predictions. Before The War, there were a number of exercises that were run in the event of a flu pandemic or a chemical and biological terrorist attack, and the effects that it would have on the population. What no one counted on was the wholesale breakdown of society that happened after the Cromwell.

I was in the Ops room in Permanent Joint Head Quarters in Northwood, having been sent there by CDS to help co-ordinate Senlac. We knew that things were starting to come to a head as there had been a near constant climb in the rate of incidents and the Sanitation Teams were working flat out. It was pretty obvious that things were going to go pear-shaped soon.

The week before Cromwell we had sent out the Warning Orders for Senlac which identified exactly what each unit in the entire British military was expected to do. We had been moving supplies around since the altercation with the Government the year before and we felt that we were in a fairly strong position. How little we knew. There is an old saying "No plan survives contact with the enemy" and in this case, that was absolutely spot on. Only this time the enemy wasn't the Soviets or the Taliban but just good old-fashioned fear and panic. We thought we had planned for every eventuality but we just didn't expect so many people to lose it so bloody quickly. We were definitely caught short.

How so?

Well for starters we couldn't mobilise fast enough. All our predictions had planned on a gradual escalation of fear in the public which would then culminate in a full-blown biblical style collapse. This would give us time to mobilise the reserves, get troops moving and start constructing defences. We had thought this would take about three weeks but instead, it happened in three days.

How did you react?

As soon as we saw that news report from America, CDS issued the full orders for Senlac. We knew that the cat was out of the bag and that things would have to get moving pretty sharpish to keep ahead of the panic. Then about an hour later there was Cromwell and the Sanitation Teams gunning down infected on the steps of a hospital in full view of the UK media. I remember turning to my staff and telling them to send out a second signal to all units, ordering them to move the start time up to the next day. I think from that point on I didn't sleep for about a month.

Can you talk me through the operation?

I'll try and give you the short version.

As I had said previously we had identified a number of defensible locations and two geographic safe zones that we could take and hold to act as bastions for as many soldiers and civilians as possible. The first stage was for pre-designated units to either, create their own fortifications or seize existing ones like castles, dig in for a siege and offer sanctuary to as many people as possible. Other units were tasked to construct the defensive lines in Scotland and Cornwall often in the face of mass migrations of panicked people and the infected that inevitably followed them.

In the three days from the Cromwell to the officially recognised start of the Panic, we had managed to capture and secure 120 of the identified locations and were in the process of getting the remaining 80 under control. It was some of the most incredible work at short notice that I have ever had the honour of witnessing. It was done with the utmost professionalism and discipline that one would expect of the British Armed Forces and I am damn proud of every one of them. Some units were so efficient that they even managed to get friends and family into the Burghs before the Panic started.

What happened once the country did panic?

Well as I am sure you remember there was just bloody chaos in that first week. The Government was paralysed with indecision, the media was fanning the flames with some of the most useless speculations and advice I have ever heard and people were understandably getting more and more terrified. It was only once we saw the complete breakdown in London as everyone tried to leave; where they all thought they were going I had no idea, but they all left anyway, that was when CDS decided to step in.

Did you attempt to contact the Government?

Of course, we did. CDS phoned the PM after Cromwell and informed him that the military had a plan and we were ready to step in and help if he would give us the order. The PM flat out refused. I think he was still miffed at us for daring to face up to him in the first place and he was convinced that it could be contained by civilian means. CDS implemented Senlac anyway and called again on the day London went into meltdown and informed him that the military was in a position to offer sanctuary and security to the population if he would announce it.

I know that today many commentators are calling what we did unconstitutional but I will always maintain that we did the right thing at the time when action was called for and damn the political niceties.

What did you do?

Well CDS called on the Queen in Windsor Castle to brief her on the situation, of course by this time the castle had become an armed camp with two Regiments in resident so she had a pretty good idea of what was going on. She grasped the situation and immediately called the Prime Minister. I don't know what was said but after that, the PM gave us official support and then, from all the accounts I have heard, went off in a sulk.

About ten minutes later we took over the Emergency Broadcasting System and began to broadcast a hastily prepared message from the Queen, which included the Balmoral Decree that threw open all Royal Estates to those who could reach and defend them, and the prepared list of Burghs. We had prepared a concise brief that informed them of where to go, what to bring and how best to survive. We kept broadcasting it all day and all night for as long as possible, updating it as the situation changed.

What was the next step?

The next stage was to get as many people to the Burghs as possible.

What about the Safe Zones?

That was the decision that will stay with me for the rest of my life. By that second week, the Safe Zone defences were still nowhere near finished. Building 30 miles of defences was no easy feat and was very time-consuming. We needed to buy them time to finish or they would have been overrun and we would have no secure base from which to resupply the Burghs and eventually recapture the country. We made the decision not to tell people about the Safe Zones until they were ready, in the hope that it would draw them and the infected elsewhere. Around 60 million people called the UK home and 99 per cent of that number were still tearing around the country in a blind panic. If they had gotten into the Safe Zones before the defences were ready that would have been it. The United Kingdom would have been reduced to a series of defended locations in a sea of infected; it would have been like the Dark Ages all over again.

So we steered people away as much as possible, held them at choke points and did our best to defend them. That was the point of this junction you know, the whole reason why 2 Mercian was here. We had recognised that unless we gave people a place to rest and stop on the way north the Scotland Safe Zone would be overrun. So we set up a refugee camp in the grounds of Allerton Castle and the Battalion dug in next to the motorway. We gave them the best defences we could find, concertina wire, bastion walls and supplies. We knew that all the infected from Liverpool, Manchester, Leeds, Birmingham and even London would be heading straight for them and we needed to hold them here for as long as possible.

What do you say to the accusations that the military abandoned those people, deliberately sacrificed them?

Look, everyone is entitled to their opinions and for those people who survived the battle or had relatives who died here, then I can understand their anger.

I guess that for all intents and purposes we did abandon those people but that was never the intention. The plan was always to evacuate them as soon as we were able. By the time we got the evacuation plan in order and the troops in place we were too late and could only save a fraction of the people left.

Could we move on, please? I have to testify in front of Parliament on this next week and I don't want to skew the testimony?

Ok. Can you tell me about the situation once the Safe Zone defences were completed?

It took about ten weeks from the first Senlac order being sent out to finish the defences. In that time the Royal Engineers had built two lines of fortifications consisting of bastion walls, ditches, moats and barbed wire that sealed the land access to Devon and northern Scotland. That was when we began the process of evacuating the refugee camps, temporary fortifications and all the refugee ships. That was a Herculean effort all by itself and the Royal Navy and RAF really earned their keep.

The real headache was the processing and clearing of all those refugees but thank God that was nothing to do with me. I was still fully focused on the defensive side of things and trying to stop the Safe Zone walls being breached.

Continental divide

RAF Lyneham

Group Captain Marcus Wilbur is the current base commander and a highly decorated officer. He spent most of The War flying the transport fleet but trained as a fast jet pilot on Typhoons. His first wartime mission was highly covert and highly dangerous and he has only recently been permitted to talk about his experience.

My squadron and I had recently relocated to RAF Kinloss as part of Op Senlac and had been glued to the television for the past month watching the world go to hell on BBC 24.

It was in early May that my wingman and I were taken to one side by John Miller, the Squadron Leader and told that we had been selected for a top-secret mission. We were told to collect our belongings and report to hanger nineteen, which was in the most isolated part of the base. We jumped into a Land Rover and drove over to be met by a bunch of grim-faced soldiers guarding the perimeter of the hanger. Of course, we were getting more and more suspicious by this point and it only got worse as we were ordered to surrender our mobile phones and our kit was searched. Once the soldiers were finished we were led to a series of small offices on the side of the hanger and told to dump our kit in the room that was clearly going to be our bedroom.

John was waiting for us in a makeshift briefing room, he greeted us and introduced the man next to him as Mike from 22 SAS. At this point, I was getting a bit concerned about what we were getting ourselves into as anything that involved those headbangers was going to be dangerous and probably damaging to someone else.

Sure enough, I wasn't disappointed. Mike began the briefing by outlining the current situation in the UK, the current rate of infection, the spread and more relevant, the refugee problem.

Refugee problem?

Yes, I had no idea either at the time. You know how when it all went to shit on the continent and how anybody who could, jumped on to a boat and made for the high seas? Well, conventional wisdom has it that most of them sailed straight past Britain and onto Iceland because we were in the middle of our Panic and Iceland was apparently cold and safe. Truth is that the Royal Navy was in the Channel, forcing ships to move on and in some cases opening fire to add some persuasion, they never sunk anything but they apparently came close to it a couple of times. You see we didn't need all these extra, possibly infected, people turning up on our shores and adding to the chaos and draining our resources. The Navy stopped that but what they couldn't stop was the swarm of refugees and infected that was crossing through the Channel Tunnel.

According to Mike, the Government had tried repeatedly to get the French to seal their end but they were either too busy or not interested, most probably both. Not really surprising seeing as they were in a worse state than we were. Not only did they have a large native population going nuts to contend with, but they also had all those refugees from the rest of Europe pouring over their borders and running for the perceived safety of the coast. I imagine that the last thing on the French Government's mind was a pipeline that was conveniently diverting loads of refugees away from Brittany and their Safe Zone. It was, however, right at the forefront of my mind as we were being informed that we would be part of the mission to close the French end.

Why the French end of the tunnel and not the British?

I asked the same question. It turns out that the original plan had called for just our end to be sealed with concrete barriers but the analysts reasoned that enough determined

70

refugees or hungry Gs could force the barricades. They couldn't take that risk so the decision was taken to seal the French end as well.

The plan was for a small SAS team to fly into France and mark the target with a laser designator, we would then drop a Paveway bomb onto the tunnel entrance and seal it. It sounds so simple doesn't it but a hundred things could go wrong.

First of all, the SAS team could be overrun, after all, we were asking them to go into a country swarming with Gs and avoid detection long enough to designate a target for us to hit; then get out again in one piece, all without getting caught by some by now very pissed off Frenchmen.

On top of that was that we were about to fly a bombing mission into another country's airspace and into the teeth of their air traffic control and military radar network. I had some serious concerns, not least of which was "Am I about to start a war with France?"

Thankfully though the SAS are nothing if not meticulous in their planning and we spent four days just working through the plan; going over every single eventuality and solving every problem that was thrown in our way. By the time we finished, we all knew the plan inside and out. After that, it was time to practice before the show and we had been given two flight simulators to play with. We spent another two days just running and running the mission until I could do it in my sleep. Thank God though because getting a bomb toss right is not easy.

What is a bomb toss?

It is the bombing technique that we had decided on for this mission. The easiest way to bomb a target was to fly over it at high altitude, release the bomb and then let it lock onto the laser and ride it all the way to the target. Problem was that we couldn't just do a high-altitude pass over France and then try to explain to the French that we just happened to be in the area when their tunnel mysteriously exploded. No, what we needed was a way of getting a bomb to the target without anyone ever knowing we were there, so a bomb toss.

The technique is quite tricky because you have to approach the target at high speed and a very low level to avoid radar detection. When you reach your release point you then pull up to about 70 degrees and release the bomb. The speed of the plane and the angle of release basically lobs the bomb in a long, high arc so that it drops straight onto the target. It's basically like an underarm throw. Quiet, efficient and more importantly; did not require me to fly straight into the French Anti-Aircraft network.

Anyway, D-Day finally came around. The SAS had left two days earlier to get into position, we were given our final brief and then the go order came from Command. My wingman and I lifted off from Kinloss just as it was starting to get dark and flew towards London for the first stage of our journey. Thankfully we were flying high so we didn't have to see the streams of refugees and infected heading north. What we could see were the fires; thousands of campfires twinkling like stars across the entire country and here and there the bonfires of a town or city burning.

It was pitch black by the time we flew over London and linked up with the refuelling tanker. We had chosen London for the meeting because the huge column of ash and soot that was still rising off the ruins was the perfect cover from French radar. It did make the fuelling process bloody difficult as we spent most of the time being buffeted around by thermals and trying to avoid sucking too much ash into our engines.

With our tanks topped off, we dropped down to 50 meters above the surface of the Thames and followed the river out into the North Sea. We shot past a number of refugee ships steaming north and then turned into the Channel. In the distance, we could see the running lights of the Royal Navy piquet line as they herded the refugee ships away from the coast.

Twenty miles out my wingman peeled off and began a slow racetrack holding pattern in the channel. He would come in for a second run if my bombs failed to hit the target. I keyed my radio "Fishing", the code word for my final approach. Seconds later came the return "Line", the laser was now active and on target.

At ten miles out I increased my speed and prepared for the toss. Five miles out I pulled the nose of the jet up and held it for two seconds before I hit the bomb release, felt the plane lighten as the Paveway was tossed into the sky and continued my roll, coming full circle and back down to the wave tops before I shot off north. I reckoned I had probably breached the French radar for about a second and then hopefully vanished.

I imagined the bomb sailing into the night sky, totally silent, no rocket motor or flame to give it away, covering five miles in a few moments as it reached the peak of its arc before the nose tipped downwards and its computer brain began sniffing for the laser mark. It would acquire its target and lock on as it began its final dive before smashing into the mouth of the tunnel and 1000 lbs of high explosives detonating in an instant and sealing it.

The net came alive again with the code word "Catch", mission accomplished. I collected my wingman and we headed for home for our post-mission analysis. According to the Squadron Leader, everything had gone according to plan and the mouth of the tunnel was now just a smoking hole in the ground. Of course, what we didn't realise was how pissed off the French were.

Apparently, they had cottoned on pretty quickly as to what had happened. Let's face it, it doesn't take the brains of an Archbishop to guess who might have blown up their nice shiny tunnel and they were pissed. Trouble was there was nothing they could do about it; there was no proof, thank

God, and both France and Britain had seen what happened with Pakistan and Iran when two nuclear nations got angry with each other. They apparently ranted and raved at what was left of our Government but ultimately realised that their only other course of action was to start a war and I think they realised that no one would benefit from that.

The only reason I am allowed to talk to you about this now is that we have all kissed and made up. We admitted what we did, apologised, paid the French for the damage and helped them rebuild the tunnel. I guess we are back to business as usual; although I doubt they will let us forget what we did, I mean look at how long it took them to get over us sinking their fleet in World War Two to stop the Nazis getting hold of it.

C'est la vie mon ami!

Axe to grind

Canterbury

Steven Maher is the chairman of the *Justice for Junction* organisation dedicated to finding the "truth" about the death of an estimated 600,000 people at Junction 47. Steven has a personal reason for this crusade, his parents died in the Allerton Castle camp during the Great Panic and he is currently campaigning for the members of the Military Command to be tried for war crimes and mass murder. He has agreed to this interview on the proviso that he be allowed to get across his view of events without any post-interview editing on my part. We are currently stood on a small hillock overlooking what used to be the Allerton Castle camp. There is very little left of the perimeter wall or the thousands of bodies that once littered the landscape. One of the Government's first acts following VB Day was to build a national memorial on the site. A one-hundred-foot-high artificial hill covers the site of the original mass grave dug by the Army during the Restoration. A beautiful stone Angel stands atop the hill looking over the single biggest loss of life in UK history.

Before we start I just want to state that the official position of Justice for Junction is that the Government and the Military deliberately abandoned hundreds of thousands of people to die so that they could save themselves.

What evidence do you have to support your claim?

It's not a "claim". It's a cold hard fact. Thousands of people did die here and the Government did nothing to help them.

Ok, but what evidence do you have?

I have the eye witness testimonies of some the survivors, the findings of the Olsen Review, UAV footage from the attacks and the archaeological evidence recovered from the camp.

Shall we start at the beginning? Could you describe the situation as your evidence describes it?

Yes, good idea, Ok.

The military's plan was to hold as many refugees as possible in one spot to act as an irresistible target to the infected which would distract them from the real prize which was the Safe Zone being constructed in Scotland. It was straight out of the pages of Redeker.

What is your response to those who say that the Redeker Plan was a necessary evil and it ultimately won The War for many nations?

I have heard that argument before, that you couldn't save everyone, like a lifeboat being capsized by too many people. It is just bullshit, why couldn't they save everyone? It's what the Government is meant to do.

What was the camp at Junction like?

Well as I said in order for the Government's plan to work the Camp needed to be appealing enough for people to want to stop running and settle in. From all the accounts I have read they spared no expense in their deception.

The entire camp covered about four square miles and had a twenty-foot-high perimeter wall. You can see remnants of it over there. **(He points to a line of collapsing gabion walls half visible in a nearby field.)**

The Army used portable bastions, these collapsible, chain link boxes that they filled with earth, to make the wall and built towers every 100m. You can see how there was no wall walk or way of seeing over so once the people were inside they could not get out again. It was like a giant trap.

But surely it is better that people don't look over the wall as that would just attract more infected.

That's just bollocks, half a million people in a camp would have made more than enough noise to attract them and that's not even mentioning the smell.

Tell me about the facilities in the camp.

Well as I said they spared no expense. After building the wall they put in tents, paths, wells, latrines, field kitchens all the like. You can just imagine how appealing it must have been to all those people. Running for their lives and all of a sudden you come across this haven where everything is provided for, it's no wonder almost everyone stopped here.

As soon as enough people arrived the Army handed over the administration and security to a hastily elected civilian committee and left. Now, the Army will say that they redeployed to help secure the Fort at Junction but I know for a fact that the vast majority of them left and drove off north.

What was the situation like with the civilian committee in charge?

Things got very bad, very quickly. Without the Army to keep control, there was a general break down of law and order. It is not surprising that with so many people crammed into a camp, living on top of each other that things degenerated so rapidly. There were fights over food, supplies, living space, almost anything you could think of. If you had something that someone else wanted, then you had to fight to keep it and that included your own dignity. The latrines backed up because no one would clean them, the wells were fouled by all the shit on the ground. That then led to rats and diseases. One of my sources survived an outbreak of Cholera that swept through the camp and killed thousands. They just dumped the bodies outside the wall and made space for more people. You remember the New Orleans flood back in 2005 and the situation in the Superdome. The camp was a hundred times worse than that. There were

77

gangs, muggings, theft, rape; the worst parts of humanity came out in this place. It must have been hell.

Every day more and more people arrived and were crammed inside. I don't know when exactly it was but at some point, the people started to trickle off and the first infected started to arrive. That was when the Army sealed people in. A JCB built a wall across the gate, sealed everyone in and then left them.

Over the course of the next few days more and more infected turned up; one of my sources told me about how he got into one of the towers to have a look around and all he could see were infected coming in from all directions, thousands of them. They were like ants, just a non-stop stream of dots coming over the horizon, arms raised, moaning, straight towards the Camp and joining a growing moat of infected.

Apparently, most of them were drawn to the fort first, I guess it was because of all the shooting and noise but there were still enough around the camp to make life hellish. It wasn't just the fear of being surrounded or under siege, although I am sure that was bad enough. It was the moaning that drove everyone mad. I take it you've been under siege at some point, heard that constant non-stop moan. It's bad enough when it is only one or two, even a couple of hundred infected doing it but when you have a million-infected moaning at you for a month. That would drive anyone mad.

What were the effects?

Have you read the reports on how the moan is one of the infected's most potent psychological weapons? The US military did studies on the effects; sleep deprivation, stress, and anxiety. All that in a frightened population of 600,000 people.

There were more fights, murders, the number of suicides shot up. Some people even threw themselves over the wall.

There are even reports of people turning into Quislings and attacking people in the camp before being put down.

It was not too bad until the Fort was overrun, that was the final straw. After a month of being under siege from only a small percentage of the horde, the remainder then turned their attention to the camp and that was when the decision to run was made.

Who made the decision?

No one knows I doubt there was any form of vote. In my opinion, some idiot just decided to go for it and the other people were so frightened that they went along with it.

What was their plan?

No idea, as far as any of my sources can tell me the first they knew about it was when the screaming started. It appears that they tried to climb over the wall by building a ramp to the top, the only problem was that as soon as it was built thousands of people surged to the top and the wall collapsed into the moat. The fucking geniuses created a walkway straight in camp and the dead came pouring in.

I don't even want to imagine what it must have been like. A million infected pouring into a contained space with 600,000 people trapped inside, it must have been a slaughter. People panicked, ran, tried to fight, tried to hide, but it did them no good as there was nowhere to run to.

I managed to get a clip from a UAV released by the military last year. They'd had a drone circling the camp for weeks and it caught the moment when the wall was breached. I don't know if you've seen it but it was like a dam breaking in slow motion. It was like a grey wave of zombies spreading out from the breach and all the people running away from it to the far side of the Camp before they were trapped against the wall and killed. It was horrible, I felt so helpless just watching it, imagine what it must have been like trapped against that wall watching as the horde ate its way toward you, knowing there was nothing you could do. I think of my parents and whether they suffered through that or died before the wall was breached. That's why I can never forgive the military if they had stayed and fought they could have saved all those people, saved my parents.

Was that the end of it?

No, and the next bit is why I think it was planned all along. The Military bombed the camp.

Really, that was never reported?

Of course not, the only reason I knew about it was from one of the survivors. He had managed to get on top of the wall and lay there waiting for an opportunity to run. He told me how he lay there listening to all those people being slaughtered and then eaten before he could leave. Apparently, he waited until most of the infected were inside the camp before jumping off the wall and running north as fast as he could.

He had gotten about a few miles away when he heard jet engines; he told me that he saw six jets flying low and slowly straight towards the camp. As they flew over he saw them dropping loads of bombs which then blew up into these huge fireballs, covering the camp.

That's why I think it was a conspiracy, get all those zombies into one place and then napalm them. Take out a million of them in one go and prevent all those that had just died from reanimating.

What makes you think it was napalm?

My source says he saw some of them wandering around on fire before they eventually collapsed. Now it takes a lot to get a human body burning and only napalm could stick to one long enough to kill it.

Let me see if I can sum up your official position? You believe that the Government and the military deliberately herded people into a contained area with the express purpose of using them as bait to keep the infected away from the northern Safe Zone. Then they waited until the camp was overrun before launching an air strike to kill as many zombies as possible.

That's correct.

Despite the valiant efforts of 2 Mercian in defence of the camp and the relief column that was only two miles away when the wall was breached.

Yes.

What do you hope to gain by pressing this course of action?

I want to bring the perpetrators of the biggest mass murder in British history to justice.

Don't you think that could be construed as a little ungrateful towards the military that protected you while you were safe in Dover Castle?

This interview is over.

Rally to the Colours

Bath

The St John's Hospice for Feral Children is located in the centre of Bath near to the historic Roman baths and hot springs and has been caring for feral individuals since the end of the war. By VB Day there were over fifty hospices spread throughout the country, today there are less than five. This is down to a combination of cost, political will, successful rehabilitation but most important is the loss of public interest.

The subject of my interview is Corporal John Smith, not his real name but one given to him by the staff since the vast majority of military records from before The War was lost. Corporal Smith is the sole survivor of 2 Mercian and the Battle of Junction. He was found during the Restoration, living in the burnt-out ruins of a church near Buckden in the Yorkshire Dales. He was wearing the tattered remains of his uniform and had the Regimental and Queens Colours tied around his waist. It is believed by the staff that he had been living alone and traumatised from the events at Junction for three years before he was found and that it was this isolation that led to his loss of speech.

For the last four years, Dr Diana Carlson has been counselling John and trying to encourage him to speak. As an interim measure Corporal Smith has been taught sign language which he will use for this interview. For clarity I have written this interview as if it were between Corporal Smith and me, although in reality, Dr Carlson is translating, I have also taken the liberty of clarifying the conversation for ease of reading.

I had been in the regiment for three years before the outbreak of the war. I had been to Afghanistan before we all pulled out and had been based in Catterick before the Panic. About three months before the battle we were getting

82

warnings from the Commanding Officer that we should standby for deployment. We had all been watching the news and had seen all the bad things going on, everyone thought we would be deployed soon and have to do some fighting.

When did you get the orders to move?

It was right after the Cromwell. I had been in the Junior Ranks Bar with my Platoon watching it live on the news. Then the Platoon Commander came in grabbed the Platoon Sergeant and started to talk to him in a corner of the bar. When he finished the Sergeant nodded and turn round, we could see him building up steam for some shouting and half of us were out of our seats ready to go. The Sergeant yelled out that we were being mobilised and had ten minutes to grab our kit and get on the parade square.

That's not a lot of time?

We had all packed our kit days before, it was just a case of running to your room, changing your uniform, grabbing your kit and getting back down to the square. Once we were there we were issued our weapons, I was a Light Machine Gunner usually but I was issued my rifle instead which I was quite surprised about. We were given lots of ammunition but no grenades or anything else which was confusing for a lot of us. We were also told to hand our helmets, body armour and NBC kit into the stores. All our mobiles were confiscated as well.

We were all there on the square, milling around in our Companies, there was lots of talk about what was going on and where we were going when the Regimental Sergeant Major came onto the square and yelled for us to form up. Pretty soon the Commanding Officer came down and briefed us on the situation. He said that the dead really were coming back to life and that we would be fully briefed by our Company Commanders. He said that we were being tasked to move south and hold a choke point in order to save as many civilians as possible. His final point was that the Army realised that there would be major fears about the safety of our families but that we shouldn't worry, the Regimental Welfare Officer was in the process of contacting all our families and getting them to a safe area. That was a big weight off all our minds.

We were told to gather around our Company Commanders who briefed us on the infected and where we were off to. He told us that we were going to a position by the A1 and we would be helping to build a fort that we would defend against any enemy that turned up. This would allow any refugees fleeing north to get away.

Pretty much as soon as the briefs had stopped a load of coaches turned up and we began to get on board. My coach joined a big convoy of vehicles, Army trucks loaded with supplies, Land Rovers with radios and tents and all the stuff the CO obviously thought we needed.

It took an hour and a half to travel to Junction 47 in a huge convoy of vehicles. We got there by about five O'clock in the afternoon and then sat around waiting in the car park of a golf driving range just off the motorway for about two hours. According to my Platoon Commander, they were marking out the perimeter of the camp, which was basically the perimeter road of the driving range.

Eventually, we were called off the coach and led to the place where we would be living. There was nothing there except a pile of canvas and military cot beds that had been dumped by the storemen. We were divided up into our sections and tasked with various jobs. One section put up the tent and set up the accommodation for the Platoon, the other section went out beyond the perimeter to stand guard and my section started to dig the outer ditch.

The engineers had marked out a perimeter about a kilometre long with flags and white tape to mark the width of the ditch. They had also dumped a load of bastions which we were told to fill in. The plan was for there to be an outer ditch two meters deep by three wide, there would then be a mound of soil from the ditch and a barrier of bastions on top. It all sounded great except we were the bastards who had to dig it, the Engineer tractor with the digging arms was busy building the civilian camp over the road, so we were left to get on with it.

It took six days, rotating between digging, guarding and sleeping, to get the outer perimeter built. Everyone got involved, sergeants and officers, to get the job done. Don't believe the press that officers never get their hands dirty, they were right there with us digging in and leading from the front.

Of course, once the wall was done the work didn't finish as we had to make it as defensible as possible. There were a lot of trees right in front of the camp that needed to be cleared and guess who had to chop them down. Then there were the work parties to help set up the camp and get things neat and tidy; things like an ammo store, cookhouse, a headquarters, latrines all that sort of stuff. We even converted the driving range into a final fall-back position, stocking it with food and ammo and defences.

By the time we finished almost two weeks later, we had a well prepared and fortified position. We had created a tangled barrier of trees and barbed wire then a cleared area, then the ditch and the wall. We felt good about our position and how long we could last but then the boredom kicked in and we had time to think.

People started to ask about their families and wanted to call them. After a lot of pressure from the soldiers, we were eventually allowed to use our mobiles to try and make calls. It didn't do any good though, we didn't realise that the country was going through the Great Panic and the mobile networks were overloaded, there was no way we could get through to anyone. Pretty soon everyone started to feel a real sense of isolation and the Commanding Officer ordered radios to be set up and tuned into the BBC, he set up film nights, sports competitions, wrestling matches, anything to keep people busy.

A huge portion of our time was spent training and patrolling. We mounted foot patrols around the perimeter going out for a day and then back in the evening. I don't think there was any point apart from to keep people busy.

Did you come across any infected at that stage?

We came across a few but they were still mostly in the cities at that point, we would shoot them, then bury the bodies and move on. If we came across any refugees we directed them to the Camp.

You said you were doing some training?

Yes, we spent a lot of time on the wall practising shooting at these wooden targets that had been set up. It was so we could get used to a headshot which was very difficult at first. The Army had trained us to aim for the centre of mass, basically the chest, but now we had to hit a small moving target. It took a lot of time and ammo but we got better and better each day.

How long was it before the infected started to turn up en mass?

It was about two weeks after the Mall that we started to see more and more refugees turning up at the Camp. They had come from all over; Manchester, Liverpool, Hull, and Birmingham even some from London, hundreds of them and more came every day. The Commanding officer realised pretty soon that the infected would not be far behind so we doubled our patrols to eliminate the ones in the lead and hopefully give us more time before the main swarms arrived.

Within a couple of days, we ran into more Gs on the patrols, sometimes it was so many that we had to fall back to the Fort, fighting a running battle the whole way before we killed them all. It was around then that we sighted the first of the major swarms coming in from the south-west. The order to

"Stand To" was passed and we all rushed to our positions on the wall. My section was stationed on the south wall facing the road and fields beyond it. The first ones I saw were just individual dots, appearing over the horizon but getting bigger every moment as they headed straight for us. Behind them more and more started to appear. Before long it looked like there was a stream of them flowing towards us, then it became a river, then a flood, just this mass of grey bodies stretching back as far as the eye could see. **The official military estimate for the size of the swarm is 1.5 million.**

It took a couple of hours for them to reach us but we could hear them way before then. The moan of God knows how many infected was carried to us by the wind and scared the crap out of us. I guess we knew then that none of us were getting out of this one.

The first to reach us were dealt with quickly by the sharpshooters in the towers out at a distance of eight hundred meters or so but then the numbers started to thicken and there were too many for them to take down, that was where we started to join in. I took my first shot at the three-hundred-meter marker. I lined up my sights on a G, this teenage girl in a tracksuit, half her face was hanging off and there was a big bite mark on her throat. I was shaking as I fired and shot the guy behind her in the chest. He pitched backwards but then got straight back up again and carried on. I calmed my nerves as everyone else around me started to open fire and this time got her right in the head. After that it was automatic, sight and shoot, reload your magazines. We each had a box of ammunition at our feet, I think it was supposed to last for a few days but I emptied mine in the first few hours.

All the time we were firing the horde was getting closer and closer, at two hundred meters the leading edges of the swarm hit the line of trees, pits and barbwire that we had laid out to try and slow them down. It worked for about an hour as G after G got tangled up or fell in a pit, but then the next one would come along, fall in the same pit, then another and pretty soon the pit was full and the next G just walked straight over the top and into the open ground.

We kept firing as more and more came through onto the open ground, some even made it to the ditch before we took them down, it was then that the order of "Fire On" came down the net. We had each been issued with a flare in preparation and now we put our rifles to one side and fired our flares at the open ground. Within seconds huge flames had leapt up from the ground. We had spent the last two weeks soaking it with diesel and napalm and now the whole thing went up in a huge blast of flame. The heat was incredible and forced us to duck behind the wall. We all cheered as we saw Gs stumbling about on fire and collapsing into pools of burning fuel, we laughed as more and more came through the trees, which had now caught fire, and walked straight into the flames, burned and collapsed. Then we saw that some just kept on coming, fell into the ditch and kept trying to crawl up to us before they eventually burnt and died. Through the flames, we could see how many more there were still coming towards us. We could see this long snake of millions of Gs stretching back as far as the horizon.

That was when the airstrikes came in; dozens of Harriers, Tornados and Typhoons, even C-130s came in low over our heads and began bombing the tail of the snake. We could see the bombs and barrels detaching and detonating amongst the horde, blowing huge holes in the crowd but then the hole would just refill and keep on coming. Worse still we could see these twinkling flares of burning Gs that had been hit and just gotten up and marched on. That really scared us, watching enough explosive going in to flatten a mountain and it having no effect on the horde. **The usefulness of bombing hordes is a debated subject. Some argue that it is ineffective as it is very difficult to destroy the brain with an explosion, others believe that it kills enough infected to be worth the effort.**

The bombers kept coming, kept hammering the tail, we could see explosions and plumes of fire from over the horizon as they tried to thin the numbers. From our point of view, it didn't do much good as we still had God knows how many Gs to deal with who were practically knocking on our door.

Then the artillery joined in. The first we knew about it was when the first rounds came whistling over our heads and detonated about a kilometre away. The explosions threw up these huge clouds of earth and body parts but again it did nothing. I saw one G caught in a blast go cartwheeling into the air his right arm flying off in a separate direction. It came down hard on its back before rolling over and dragging itself towards us. I don't think it took them long to realise that it was having no effect and they switched to air burst detonations. This is where the shell detonates above a target and shreds it with fragments and shrapnel. It was incredible, around would come whistling in, it would detonate and then a whole swath of the swarm just dropped as if they were puppets whose strings had been cut. It was brilliant; single-handedly the artillery brought our morale back up.

I remember taking a few minutes to have a piss, reload my magazines and light a cigarette. I grabbed a quick look around to see how we were doing. It looked like something out of a horror movie and a war film merged together. There were these bloody great explosions on the horizon and jets crisscrossing the sky, artillery rounds detonating and cutting down swathes of Gs. The woods and fields around us were on fire and burning Gs were still coming for us and rapidly filling up the ditch. It was fire, smoke, the smell of burning flesh and noise, it was chaos.

I think at that point we were pretty close to being overrun but the CO had thought of that too. I looked back into the camp to see the Quarter Master and his team driving a fuel truck up to the wall where the Gs were thickest and running the hose over the wall. They started up the pump and a stream of diesel went over the wall and into the ditch and the mass of Gs stuck in there. It must have been ten minutes or so before they stopped and drove off to the next part of the wall and started up again. All that time we were back at the wall firing away cutting down those in the ditch and in the open ground. Then we were told to get down, I was a little bit slower than my mates and I got caught in the face by the wall of fire that came racing down the ditch. That's how I got this. **He points to a large burn scar on the left side of his face.**

I woke up in the Aid Post with half my head bandaged. It was night and I couldn't hear any firing only the moan of the Gs. I grabbed one of the medics and asked what was going on. He told me that the CO had flooded the ditch with fuel and it was burning up all the Gs that fell in the ditch effectively putting another barrier between us and them. The CO had ordered half the men off the wall to rest and set about preparing for the long haul. I found out later that we had suffered no casualties and held off over a million infected. But it was just the first day.

We managed to hold them off for another month before the walls were eventually breached. Thank God for the RAF. They flew in supplies daily; food, water, ammunition but most importantly fuel. It was the only thing keeping the fires in the ditch going, we must have poured millions of gallons in there. We realised fairly quickly though that we did not need a raging inferno the whole time, we just needed to keep it hot enough to start their flesh burning once they fell in the ditch and incinerate them while they were in there. Every few hours we would turn on the taps and get the BBQ going again if we thought the pile was getting too high. That was pretty much the routine for the first three weeks, we would rest, as much as was possible with millions of zombies moaning away, we would shoot those that were in danger of getting over the wall and we would keep the fire going. It actually got a bit boring at times.

Then in the last week, the helicopters of fuel and the supply drops stopped coming, and the fires began to die down. Within two days of the last helicopter the fuel ran out and a few hours later the fire went out. That was when every man was called to the wall and we went back into it again. Our orders were to fire at everything in the open ground to try and keep them away from the walls and the ditch.

By now the open ground was littered with mounds of burn corpses which had helped to slow down their advance, but now they were getting closer and those in the ditch were starting to fill it up, within a day there was a carpet of bodies from the wood line to the base of the mound. They kept coming and the more we killed at the base of the mound the larger the pile got until there was a sloping ramp of corpses right up to the base of the wall.

We could have held them like that for days. They would try to climb up but we would shot them and they would tumble back down, taking out a couple of their friends if you were lucky but then the ammo ran out. It happened on the fourth day of that final week, the last rifle fired its last shot and we were down to hand to hand.

We never thought it would get to this point so he didn't have anything decent to fight with. We were all carrying a mixture of pick handles, spades, tent poles and our entrenching tools. We had to stand at our wall and wait for them to come to us before we would smash their heads and push them back down the other side. After that it was just a matter of attrition, I think everyone knew it, you could see men looking for a way out, except there wasn't one. We were completely surrounded and cut off.

Pretty soon the exhaustion kicked in. Men would miss time a swing and then the G would be on him, his mates would finish it off and it was one less man at the wall for the next time.

The end when it came happened really quickly. A section of the wall on the eastern side collapsed and the Gs came pouring in. I remember watching as the men rushed to fill the breach before being overwhelmed. Someone yelled to get to the Citadel at the driving range, and we all fell back and ran as fast as we could. I was one of the first there and clambered over the bastions we had placed on the stairs to the top deck. I turned and started to pull people over but pretty soon it turned into a mad scrum as the men fought each other to get over. Behind them came the Gs. Some of the men at the rear turned to fight them before being dragged down and torn apart. I watched a friend of mine who I had been through training with, take down three of them with a pickaxe before he was killed.

In the end, it was me, a few other soldiers and the Commanding Officer. We knew that there was no hope of escape and had decided to keep as many of them focused on us as possible before we were overrun. We each took turns at the barricade, leaning over to crack as many skulls as possible but we kept being whittled down as people were bitten or grabbed and dragged over the barricade.

In the end, there was the Commanding Officer, a sergeant and me. The Commanding Officer took me to one side and told me that he wanted me to take the Colours and get them to safety. I asked him how I was going to do that surrounded by millions of Gs. His plan was to get me onto the roof of the driving range and then I was to keep quiet, wait till they moved off to attack the civilian camp and then make a run for it and get the Colours to Scotland. I said that I wanted to stay and do my duty but he told me that my duty now was to survive and tell people what had happened here.

In the end, he had to order me to do it. We pulled the Colours off their poles and folded them carefully inside a waterproof bag before they hoisted me and a backpack of rations onto the roof. I lay there silently as I heard the CO turn to the sergeant and say "shall we" before they both went down the stairs to take the fight to the enemy.

How long did you have to wait?

It took three days for the camp to empty as they headed off to surround the civilians. I was left with a couple of hundred stragglers who saw me as soon as I rolled off the roof and onto the top floor of the driving range. I didn't hang around and jumped to the ground and ran for the wall. They turned and started to chase me, grab for me when they got close. I made it onto the wall and half ran half slid down the mound of corpses piled against it. I ran as far as I could before collapsing. I can't really remember anything else after that, I'm sorry.

It's Ok it's been a really good story, thank you.

You will make sure people know they died heroes?

Of course, but I think most people already know that.

Good, then I've done my duty.

Authors note: Corporal John Smith died peacefully in his sleep two months after this interview. In accordance with his wishes, he was cremated and his ashes scattered across the site of the Junction 47 fort, he said it was "so he could be with his mates". Should you wish to see the Colours Corporal John saved, they currently hang in St George's Chapel in Windsor Castle.

Flight to safety

Exeter, Devon

Josh Peck is a helicopter pilot for the local Militia providing surveillance of the coastline and rapid response to any incursion from the sea. This is a job he is ideally suited for given that he was a news helicopter pilot before the war.

Did you ever drive down the A303 on a Friday before the war? No, lucky you. The thing was a bloody nightmare. It was probably one of the dumbest designs for a road ever. The first part was a dual carriageway which then narrowed down to a single lane right by Stone Henge. Fucking genius. Let's take a busy road and narrow it down right by one of the most popular tourist points in the country, no wonder it was bloody congested. I used to live around there and every Friday the world and its entire family would try to get down to the west country for the weekend and every Friday thousands of cars would hurtle along the A303 and hit the biggest traffic jam in existence.

If you can imagine how bad it was before The War when it was only tourists and weekend caravaners, then imagine what it was like when half of western England was madly trying to get to safety. I was still flying the news chopper at that point and was covering the mass exodus from London with the anchorwoman from the station. We were flying down the M3 following this sea of people all of whom had just been told about the Safe Zones being opened in Scotland and Devon and were literally running or driving for their lives.

The editor had told us to fly down the route of the evacuation shooting as we went and then get pictures of the Safe Zone wall before landing in Exeter where he would meet us. We flew down the M3 which was fairly clear. There was the odd car or truck abandoned by the side of the road, a couple of car crashes that must have been caused in the first few weeks of the Panic and a few cars that were racing down the motorway. It was only when we turned off the M3 and started to follow the A303 that we could see that things had gone really wrong.

There was just a sea of cars tailing back to near Andover. They were bumper to bumper and packed so tight that people were climbing through windows or sunroofs to get out. There were people who were just sitting in their cars waiting, that was just so bloody British, sitting there hoping the traffic would move and not wanting to make a fuss. The thing that we could see that they couldn't was that there were cars all the way to the horizon and nothing was moving. Cars were clogging both lanes and there were people walking either side of the road carrying as much as they could. We saw campsites springing up on hills and people fighting over the best spots or the safest. And from the direction of all the major towns and cities came the infected.

We could see them in ones or twos just heading over the fields for this great snake of people. It must have been like an all you could eat buffet for them. I saw a group of them hit the side of the road near Wincanton and watched people scatter in all directions just fleeing into the countryside. Those were the lucky ones. Others were pinned against the cars and dragged down.

We caught it all on camera as this family of five tried to climb over the cars to get away. The parents got caught by their legs as they tried to get on the roof of a Volvo and were dragged back into the swarm. The three kids made it along the cars for a while, until one of them fell into an open sunroof and a G went straight in after her, we could see the car rocking back and forth and these bloody handprints being smeared on the windows. The remaining two went back to help but one of them was grabbed by a G that had been stuck in a car passenger seat. It got the kid by the arm and just pulled him into the car. The poor bastard was dragged in head first and we could see his sister pulling on his feet while he was kicking and screaming. The last shot we got as we flew on was this terrified little girl kneeling on the bonnet of a car holding her brother's shoe sobbing and frozen in fear. I wanted to fly down and save her but the anchor was having none of it, I guess she thought we would be swamped by people as soon as we started to descend.

I still see her face though. I should have done something, anything.

It got worse as we got closer to the wall. The numbers of people started to increase but they didn't seem to be going anywhere, just waiting, looking around in fear for the infected that would inevitably turn up. Then we saw why.

The wall was massive and stretched from horizon to horizon and looked like something the Romans would have built.

Can you describe it for me?

It was a series of ditches and mounds cutting across the landscape like a muddy scar. The first two ditches were only about a meter deep with a meter-high mound on the other side, each mound had coils of barbed wire running along the top. Then there was a stretch of open ground and the main wall. There was a really big ditch in front of the wall, probably around three meters deep and then a mound of the same height with a long line of those earth-filled boxes on top.

They had been stacked to create a wall about twenty meters high with a walkway built in so that soldiers could stand on the top. There were these watch towers as well that had been built out of scaffolding and we could see soldiers manning those as well.

Were they letting people in?

Yeah, but it was a really slow process. There was a major gate wherever the wall crossed a main road but there were just too many people trying to push their way in. The Army was being pretty ruthless about it though. They were letting small groups of people through at a time and making them walk past these dog cages one by one. Sometimes the dogs did nothing but other times they went nuts, throwing themselves at the cages and barking like crazy. We watched as those the dogs barked at were led away to a separate fenced off camp and locked in. The rest were loaded onto trucks and driven off to the west.

We must have spent twenty minutes or so filming this mass of people before this huge swarm of infected turned up and people just went crazy. They surged towards the gate, pushing and shoving. People were trampled and crushed in the panic but I think some people managed to get through before the soldiers sealed the gate. It was like something out of a medieval castle you know, this huge drawbridge just started to lift away from the ditch with people still on it, some people at the front of the crowd managed to jump and hang on long enough to slide down the other side but the vast majority were pushed into the ditch by the crowd. People were spreading out down the ditch trying to climb up the mound and banging away on the walls screaming to be let in. I saw soldiers throwing ropes over the wall and hauling people up but it was so few. Then the infected hit the crowd and the killing began. People ran for their lives but got tangled in the barbwire, left there helpless as the Gs closed in on them and began to feed. Within minutes the space in front of the gate had been turned into a charnel house with feeding zombies and fleeing civilians.

We watched for as long as we could before an attack helicopter appeared and ordered us to follow them to a landing area. We didn't really have much of a choice in the matter; a big gun pointing at you can be very persuasive, besides I think we had all seen about as much as we could stomach.

We were escorted to Exeter airport flying over a landscape dotted with refugee camps and touched down off the main runway. We were met by an Army Major and a squad of soldiers who welcomed us to the Safe Zone, the news crew

97

were led away and I think sent to one of the refugee camps and my co-pilot and I were conscripted. No pomp, no ceremony, we were just told: "Welcome to the army" by a smiling Major and a squad of soldiers, not really a lot you can say to an offer like that. But I can't complain we were in the Safe Zone and for the first time in three months, I felt safe.

CONSOLIDATION

Resources

Hever Castle, Kent

Set in the beautiful English countryside, Hever Castle was most well known for being the childhood home of Anne Boleyn, the second wife of King Henry VIII. In the pre-War years, it was a popular tourist attraction but throughout the War, the castle was home to a small band of survivors who lived in relative safety and comfort thanks to the deep moat and extensive vegetable gardens.

Hever Castle is now the home of Lord James McMillan. In the years before the War, Lord McMillan was a successful businessman running a well-known chain of high street clothing stores. When the Panic hit he managed to evacuate his entire family and many friends to his estate in Scotland where he helped to feed and relocate many refugees. It was this philanthropic effort which brought him to the notice of the Government. He was offered the newly created job of Minister for Resources, a role he held throughout The War before becoming Chancellor of the Exchequer, the position he still holds today.

I was offered the role of Minister for Resources a few weeks after the Royalist Movement trounced the politicians. I was at my estate near Crieff and was trying to organising all the refugees that I suddenly found on my doorstep when a helicopter came in and landed on what was left of my front lawn. Most of it was by then in the process of being converted into veg gardens. I was in my study and in the middle of a full-blown row with one of the estate's farmers, who didn't want his prime Aberdeen Angus cows moved off their grassland and slaughtered. I was trying to get across the point that for the resources that one herd takes up I

100

could feed hundreds of people. I was so engrossed in the argument that I barely registered the helicopter, nor the two soldiers who stood in the doorway to my office. It was only when one of them yelled "Make way for the Prince Regent" that I stopped shouting and took notice.

I had no idea how long the Prince had been standing there but he had obviously heard enough as he had a slight smile on his face. He turned to an aide standing by his side and said: "He's the one, he will be perfect". After recovering from my initial shock, I asked what he meant, the Prince replied that he needed someone to organise the Safe Zones and get the country on to a war footing and from what he had just seen I was the perfect man for the job.

What did you say?

I said yes, of course, you don't say no to the deputy head of the country when he asks you to help save it.

When did you start?

That was my next question. The Prince smiled and said "Now", then told me to join him on the helicopter. I said a quick goodbye to my wife, turned over management of the estate to her then got in the helicopter and took off. The Prince was straight down to business; he briefed me in the air en-route to the new seat of Government at Balmoral and explained the situation in the country as he saw it and what needed to be done. It was only then that the enormity of the task before me became obvious.

Can you explain his view?

The short version was that things were in a pretty sorry state; some sixty per cent of the population was either dead or undead. The remaining forty per cent were either in the Safe Zones, Burghs, on ships off the coast or hiding in The Grey. There was precious little food available, no industrial base to call on, supplies of oil, gas and petrol were dwindling and we were basically in danger of sliding back into the Dark Ages. On top of all this was the fact that the Safe Zones were not even fully clear yet, the military was still conducting "Sanitation Operations" and every day brought fresh sightings of the infected. All this the Prince relayed to me in such a clear and calm way that he made it seem like it was just a small snafu and everything would sort itself out. It really gave me a confidence boost knowing I had his support. I know he had gotten a lot of stick in the past but when the chips were down the Prince and the Royal Family as a whole, showed their true colours. They gave everything to ensure the survival of this country and I watched a true servant of the people work himself to the bone so that others could have a better life and a chance at survival, "Cometh the hour, cometh the man" as they say.

Where did you start with such a massive task?

Well, I began with the refugee camps. There was something like three hundred in the northern zone alone and every one of them was a huge drain on resources; food, guards, water, power, everything. They had to be emptied and fast.

Before that, though we had to find places to send them and so we began the census. It was probably the most meticulous survey of the state of a nation since The Doomsday Book in 1086 and was appropriately nick-named The Armageddon Census. We recruited four thousand volunteers from the camps, gave them each a bicycle and sent them out into both Safe Zones to begin their work. They counted everything; the number of people, their names, where they lived, even if that was a tent in a camp and what skills if any, they had. What possessions, equipment and supplies were available, how many rooms a house had, what houses were empty, what factories were working and what they could produce. Basically, anything that could be counted or surveyed was.

All of it was catalogued and the results collated by another group of volunteers into a huge database run out of a small room in Balmoral Castle. That was the heart of my empire, a series of rooms in one wing, staffed by about a hundred-people drawn from all walks of life. I had ex-military, farmers, members of the Red Cross, even a lady from the Women's Institute, anyone who had any knowledge of marshalling and organising resources found themselves working for me.

Our next biggest challenge was time. Winter was coming and all of the meteorological data pointed towards it being a really harsh one, we were running out of resources and people were still dying, we had to act fast. The surveyors had been given just two weeks to gather their information and get it back to "The Ministry". The computer geeks then had another two weeks to collate it and I had about ten minutes to work out what we were going to do with all that information.

What was your first step?

As I said, the first priority was to empty the camps. During the survey everyone had been asked about their skills and former jobs, this was recorded and each person was given a card with a grade on it. The three grades were based on how useful we considered people to be. P1s were people who had a useable skill; an ex-soldier, a farmer, gunsmith, blacksmith, anything that could be used to improve the situation. P2s were people who could be used as administrators and coordinators and P3s were the unskilled labour and as you can imagine there were a lot more of the latter two than the first. You have no idea some of the jobs that were listed as skills; manager of this, coordinator of that, all perfectly suited to the pre-war, post-industrial society that we all used to be part of but absolutely sod all use in the current situation. Some of the local council ones were the best; my favourite was "Walking Co-ordinator". We used to have a pinboard with some of the most amusing jobs ranked on it, a bit mean I grant you but it kept morale up.

Anyway, as I said we had to get these people working and housed fast, so we set up housing offices in each camp, staffed by the P2s and used the data the survey had collated to find people new homes. We put people wherever we could. Most of the time it was in empty houses but some of the time it was in houses that were already occupied. There were a lot of people who were not happy about that but needs must. People needed a roof over their head and if one family had a large enough house they doubled up. It didn't always work and sometimes people had to be moved to prevent them from killing one another but more often than not they knuckled down and got on with it.

The next step was getting people working and this was a top priority, not just because we had lots of work that needed doing but because it helped people to deal with the shock and trauma of everything that had happened. We didn't know why at the time but people were still dying, just going to bed at night and not waking up. We thought that work would help keep people's minds off their troubles, give them a reason to get up in the morning.

There was so much that needed to be done in those first months and I barely slept for most of it. We had to clear streets of rubble, get roads and rail lines reopened, bodies burnt, God there were so many of those. There was the harvest that had to be brought in and a myriad of other jobs, fortunately though we had a vast pool of labour to draw on.

The P1s were all busy setting up their relevant industries with whatever resources we could give them. If a blacksmith needed iron to make nails, we found it for him but more importantly, we gave them apprentices and I considered this to be our most valuable resource. It was my hope that by training as many people as possible in useful skills we could scatter them across the Safe Zones and make towns and villages as self-sufficient as possible and therefore less reliant on Government aid.

At the same time, the best of the P2s were being drafted into the new Civil Service and the P3s were being used for all that unskilled but physical labour that needed doing.

Of course, once all those manual labour jobs ran out we had to find things for the P3s to do and that was where the civilian retraining program came in. We formed training teams made up of P1s all of whom had different skills. We made sure each team had at least one farmer or gardener to teach people how to grow their own food. There was a soldier to advise on defence and security, a plumber, electrician and builder to give people the practical skills and a medic or where possible a doctor to train people on basic first aid and health. We sent them to every settlement in the Safe Zones and they would stay as long as they felt was necessary to get that place on its feet before moving on. It was really heartening to see these people from different parts of the country come together and begin to form a new society, it really helped to bond people together.

I know a lot of countries had similar problems to us when it came to harnessing their workforce but we also had the additional burden of a vast Welfare State. It seems so alien to us today how anyone would want to be a drain on society, not working and not contributing but just sitting at home watching daytime TV and bleeding money from the Government. Thank God that's gone the way of the Dodo and people work hard, contribute and support themselves. But back then we had a whole swathe of society that expected everything to be done for them; even after having seen the world essentially end they were not prepared to do anything about it and expected the Government to sort it out for them. It was so bloody frustrating. Not everyone was like that I hasten to add but there were enough to make life bloody difficult.

What about food, surely that was in short supply?

Actually, we weren't too bad off when it came to food. The Panic had started in the first half of the year after the spring plantings had taken place, it was now late summer and near harvest time so we had a vast amount of grain and vegetables in the fields ready to go. What we lacked were people to harvest it. There was a chronic shortage of fuel for the farm vehicles so the entire harvest had to be done by hand. The solution was to essentially "collectivise" the farms and turned them into communes under central Government control. We moved people from the camps to the farms and created a chain of command to help run the settlement. The farmer was the subject matter expert, there was a civil servant on hand to act as an administrator and coordinate the effort and there was a police officer to help coordinate security and keep order.

I got a lot of stick for that idea and had to fight the Prince pretty hard to get the bill signed. It's not really surprising when you consider that on the surface it looked like we were selling people into a modern form of serfdom but looking back in hindsight you can see how well it worked. It brought people together, gave them a sense of community and purpose and gave them a reason to carry on. We always moved people as families and on every farm, I visited I met people who were genuinely happy with their situation. You just have to look at how many families have settled on their original farms to see that it worked. Sorry if that seems a bit defensive but as I said I got a lot of grief.

Anyway, the harvest came in and people had enough of the bare essentials to survive the winter but it was two factors that helped to feed the population, the first was the Dig for Victory campaign and the second was Vertical Farms.

The former was essentially a rehashing of the World War II policy of turning every square inch of available ground over to food production, everything from vegetables and chickens to goats and pigs. It was surprisingly easy to implement as in the years leading up to The War there had been a growing trend throughout the country for growing your own food, the upside of which was a pool of knowledge in almost every town that could be harnessed for the community. It was fantastic and by the following summer allowed almost every town to become self-sufficient in terms of food.

However, the real life saver was Vertical Farming. Essentially this was the idea of growing food by using hydroponics in a controlled environment while making use of all available space. The advantage of this technique was that we could grow large amounts of any type of food, all year round. The real drivers of this program were a team of agricultural students from Edinburgh who had been running a prototype system in an old cattle shed on the outskirts of the city. I got a quick tour and once I saw how they were growing four acres worth of tomatoes in a one-hundred-meter-long shed I told them their trial was approved and they could have whatever they needed. Sadly, that wasn't very much, a few trucks and some workers but what I could give them was a licence to take over empty buildings and first dibs on whatever salvage they could find.

I was genuinely amazed at what they achieved, within weeks they had their second site up and running in an abandoned warehouse in Edinburgh having built a system out of office furniture, plumbing supplies and strip lighting. It was a bit of a struggle at first but once the country started to get back on its feet we were able to offer them more and more support and it grew from there. By the end of the second year, we had Vertical Farms in every city and large town in the Safe Zones and had transmitted the plans to every Burgh and settlement we could reach. In my opinion, it saved this country from starvation and the guy who developed it should be given a bucket load of medals and knighted.

What about power and infrastructure?

Again, we were actually quite well off. Two of the country's nuclear power stations were in Scotland, as where a number of hydroelectric systems and offshore wind farms. We were even able to plug a few of the nuclear submarines in Faslane into the National Grid. Once we had secured the stations and got them up and running there was almost no problem with energy and thanks to the National Grid we could supply power to any part of the UK that still had a working substation. A central node was set up in Dundee that could control the flow of electricity; it essentially allowed us to supply only those areas where we knew that there was a settlement or Burgh. It may have seemed harsh to those people somehow hanging on in London or some of the other big cities but there was no way we could supply the huge demands of energy that cities that size needed. All those automatic streetlights or traffic systems, even lights or TVs left on in people's houses would have sucked up huge amounts of power, so we shut them off. I cannot stress how such a simple thing helped to save so many people, it gave hope to all of those in the Burghs or the Grey just by having something as simple as the lights back on.

With power, we could pump water, flush toilets and process sewage, although a lot of this went straight onto the fields or vegetable patches. We could talk to other parts of the country again through the National Communication Network and we could supply factories with enough energy to begin the process of salvaging resources and getting an industrial base up and running. Most importantly we could get power to the oil rigs in the North Sea and get them pumping precious oil and gas to the refinery at Grangemouth. However, even then that was not a perfect solution. In the years running up to The War, the Government had taken the decision to resume oil and gas exploration in the North Sea. Because of this, most of the wells were dangerously low and there would not be enough to meet all of the nation's needs, especially when you started to add in aviation fuel for the heavy lift aircraft and heavy oil for all the shipping, it was a real concern.

We needed a radical solution and I was open to all offers. Fortunately, I was again rescued by a group of university students who had been working on biofuels that used algae as its base. I was sold the first time they pitched it to me and within weeks we had set up the first farm on the coast. After that, the whole process just took off with almost every bit a coastline given over to algae farms and refineries.

It was a miracle. Not only did we now have a renewable form of fuel we could put in any vehicle but it created jobs and helped to move the country away from an oil-dependent economy. I am especially proud of the last part. For too long the country had been dependent on insecure foreign oil which had put us at risk in the past, now we were free of that burden and energy independent.

What can you tell me about the recycling effort?

Well as I said earlier we had almost no industrial base to draw on. In the years since World War II, Britain had become a post-industrial society and almost everything we used on a daily basis was imported from somewhere else that could produce it cheaper than we could. Obviously, when The War broke out and global trade collapsed overnight we found ourselves drastically short of everything. All the clothes that I used to sell were made in China, the TV I used to watch was made in Taiwan, even the iron that was used to produce the SA80 was imported from India. We needed to find ways to equip our soldiers, mend our machines, even simple things like finding enough nails to allow people to build homes but we just did not have the natural resources to supply all those needs. What we did have was a wealth of gadgets, consumer goods and cars in every household that were a mine of resources we could dig into. Thank God for years of Western consumerism.

We set up workshops in every town that processed everything from the steel and aluminium in cars to the copper in telephone lines, even the rare metals in plasma TVs and mobile phones were used. Everything that could be recycled was. Of course, some people objected to losing their hard-earned property but each salvage party had Government backing, plus a squad of soldiers to back them up. When the new laws about hoarding came in, we found most people came forward and gave up their goods voluntarily. Of course, the standard punishments and public humiliations helped. Nothing like a day in the stocks for a former celebrity or billionaire who is hoarding food to get the point across that we are all in this together.

The process became so efficient that we could set up a production line aimed at a single product. There was one in Dumbarton that would have cars going in one end and wind-turbines made from engine alternators and door panels coming out the other. There was another in Perth that produced nothing but cutlasses.

He gestures to the wall behind him which is festooned with weapons both ancient and modern. He is describing the signature weapon of The War in Britain, it has a blade about forty centimetres long, it starts off narrow at the hilt but widens out to a large curved chopping tip. The basket hilt is hollow which allows it to be clipped to a wooden pole and used to dispatch zombies from behind the safety of a fortification.

We made thousands of those in the first year. They were the perfect multi-tool; good for farm work, butchering animals and lopping off heads. The first batches went to the military of course but after that, we issued them to everyone, farmers and Militia first and then to everyone we could get them to. After all, there were nowhere near enough guns to go around and not enough bullets so a massive bloody meat cleaver was the next best thing to allow the population to start defending itself. Makes you feel a whole lot safer and I never went anywhere without mine, still don't.

Roundheads and Cavaliers

Oxford University, Oxfordshire

**Professor Andrew Smale is head of the Political Studies
department at Oxford University. He is a keen historian
and a widely recognised expert on the subject of this
interview, the Royalist Movement. He has written two
books on the Political impact of the Zombie War and is
halfway through his third.**

It would not be too sensational to say that the political
upheavals of the first years of the Zombie War were almost
as devastating as the English Civil War of the seventeenth
century. The early signs of the political change to come
could be seen in those first clashes between the Military
and Government before the Panic. By essentially facing up
to the Prime Minister and ignoring his direct orders to take
no action and then going ahead anyway, the Chief of the
Defence Staff had done away with hundreds of years of
political understanding; that despite no direct oaths of
loyalty to the Government, the military would follow their
orders as if they came from the Queen.

That first moment of defiance and the Government's
inability to enforce its will on the Military sowed the seeds of
its own downfall. Of course, the fact that the Military was
morally right to act as they did in no way justifies their
flagrant disregard for the proper chain of command.

**Despite the fact, their actions saved thousands of
lives?**

I don't deny that by circumventing the Government and
putting Operation Senlac into effect they saved lives. If they
had done nothing then millions more people, possibly the
entire United Kingdom would have died. I am not disputing
that they did the morally correct thing. I am arguing that they
did the politically wrong thing. Let us not forget that the
actions of the Sanitation Teams were entirely illegal.

Why was that?

To deploy soldiers on the streets of the UK without the permission of Parliament is illegal. It is as simple as that. It is an understanding that all stable democracies have as a fundamental agreement between the Military and the people they serve. The Sanitation Teams had no such mandate and were operating outside the law. Because their record is sealed for the next hundred years we will not know in this lifetime whether or not any innocent civilians were caught up in their missions.

You say the seeds were sown in those first years, when did they bloom so to speak?

It was at the beginning of the Consolidation that events began to come together. The Military had built and sealed the Safe Zones, again completely independent of any political control and was essentially running their own kingdom within the borders of the UK. I have not even touched on the Burghs which really could be construed as the Army grabbing its own independent fiefdoms.

Isn't that a bit harsh given that it was a clearly stated aim of Op Senlac to maintain control of the Safe Zones until a civilian government could be elected and that the Burghs would only be under military control until a civilian council could be formed?

I grant you that this was the stated intent but the risk, as history has shown us, with so many military coup d'état, having seized power "for the good of the nation" it is then almost impossible to get them out again.

Regardless, the situation was that the Military had control of the Safe Zones and there was no Civilian Government to contest them.

Why was there no Government?

The simple answer was that they were all dead, although that is not entirely accurate. The vast majority of the Cabinet was killed during the Panic when they were trapped in the Cabinet Office, the Prime Minister among them. Those politicians that managed to make it to the Northern Safe Zone were either Scottish MPs or former MPs whose constituencies were in the Gray and now had a significantly less vocal population.

The political parties were in chaos, busy tearing themselves apart. Added to this was the fact that the people felt let down by their politicians; they had let the Panic happen and had not acted when it was required. There was simply no one in a position to offer political guidance to a traumatised and damaged nation.

Except for the Military.

Yes, except the Military. While I don't agree with what they did, they provided the stability and security that allowed the Consolidation to happen and to their credit, they did try to form a Civilian Government from the remnants of the political parties. They put all the surviving politicians in a room in Stirling in the hope that they would come to an agreement and form a Government.

Of course, it was a bloody disaster, most politicians couldn't agree on the colour of mud and yet they were expected to agree on who should run the country. They wasted two valuable weeks trying to grab power and throw themselves into roles on party lines. I consider myself an advocate of the nobility and fairness of the democratic system but I still feel ashamed by the self-serving nature of those politicians. Added onto this was the fact that the population was deeply resentful of politicians and grateful to the Military, it is easy to see why the Royalists stepped in.

Who were the Royalists precisely?

It is actually very difficult to say. The Royalists were not a political party; they were merely people who felt that the country desperately needed leadership that was acceptable to the people. The most obvious and appropriate was the Royal Family. The Queen was held in high regard by most of the population and her actions in the Panic and generosity with the Balmoral Decree had shown that her first role was always to serve the people.

The first use of the term was I believe just after the attempt to form a government. The story goes that having lost patience with the lack of progress, the Military turned them out of the theatre and told them all to report to the job centre where they could "make themselves useful". One officer was reported to have said that he understood how the Royalists felt, referring to the English Civil War. I believe that the phrase just caught on from there but it only became a widely used term after the fact.

How did the movement gain momentum?

It actually began as a grassroots movement, which is surprising given that the term "Royalist" brings about images of elitism and class society. The first calls for change came from the soldiers in the lower ranks of the Military; many of whom had seen the political infighting first-hand and were no doubt aware of what had happened in Stirling. They began to voice more and more stridently to their officers what they felt. Why should they be expected to follow the orders of politicians who, as far as they could see, had done nothing to help the country and couldn't organise a proverbial "piss up in a brewery".

The Generals realised fairly quickly that without the support and consent of the soldiers there was no way a government could be formed and indeed the country as a whole would suffer. Those first few weeks were essentially rudderless after all, no major decisions could be made and no major appointments announced. The Generals could have taken control and formed some form of British Junta but there was the likelihood of splitting the country and inciting a civil war. To their credit, they realised they needed someone that was universally respected and that person was the Queen.

How was the Queen persuaded to take control?

A delegation of Generals, Admirals and Air Marshals first approached the Prince Regent with the intent of sounding out whether he would support the idea. From everything I have heard he had actually come to a similar conclusion but would not make a move without the consent of the monarch. The next step was to contact the Queen in Windsor and ask her permission to disband Parliament and form "an interim Royal Council to administer the realm, until such time as a new government could be formed" which she duly granted. It was a very British coup really, no guns, no one killed, lots of formal language but the government of a nation overthrown none the less.

What form did the Royal Council take?

It was a return to feudalism in its most basic form. The Queen was the head of government, as she had always been but now she had real power to run the country despite being under siege in Windsor. The Prince Regent was tasked as her deputy and because of his location in the Northern Safe Zone and his freedom to move around, the real role of administering and running the country fell to him. The Regent set up the Privy Council which consisted of the head of the Military, the Minister for Resources, Foreign Secretary and a number of other posts either filled by members of the Royal Family or high profile public figures. Below the Regent were his sons each of whom was the Governor of one of the Safe Zones, both of them with an advisory staff made up of military men and civilian experts. It was a family pyramid of power that put the country back to 1066.

You can't dispute that it was an effective form of government and that it got things done?

So is a dictatorship but that doesn't make it right. For the first year, the Royal Council ignored all of the opinions of their subjects and just ploughed ahead with their plans; the mass relocations, the collectivisation of farms, the categorising of individuals along skill lines, Stalin did less to his people. A thousand years of hard-won civil liberties swept aside. That is not to mention the new punishment laws that were brought in; flogging, stocks, public humiliation, chain gangs and hanging. It was unbelievable.

Surely you have to agree that the thinking behind the laws was sound?

I have heard this argument before, young man. That we did not have the resources to guard prisoners and why should able-bodied citizens be expected to guard other able-bodied citizens? Better to give them a short sharp punishment to make the point and then get them back to work. Yes, it all sounds very logical and process driven but the fact remains that the Royalists ran roughshod over every social development since Magna Carta.

But it got things done and more often than not for the better. What if the Government had had these powers prior to the War, it could have been prevented?

But what sort of country would we have been? North Korea had these powers and look at them, no one knows what the hell happened to their entire population, they could all be underground in a Stalinist utopia for all we know. I cannot dispute that the Royal Council got things done and for a while, people were content to go along with it on that basis but once the initial panic and relocations were over and people began to get more settled that was when they began to demand more freedoms and a return to government accountability.

What form did this change take?

The most obvious and sweeping change was through the formation of a new parliament and elections. However, this time the elected representatives were chosen from among the community. It was truly a liberating moment for many people, really knowing the person they were electing and not just ticking a name on a ballot sheet. Each settlement in the Safe Zones elected one person to represent them; this person then attended the Regional Councils. There was one of these for each Safe Zone and it was here that all the problems were discussed and solutions proposed. Whatever a Council decided on had to be ratified by the Royal Council but it allowed people to regain control over their lives again.

That was just the first step; with a Regional Government set up the Royal Council began to hand over more and more roles to the people. It was one of the beauties of the system; it identified natural leaders and people who could get things done. After all, there was no way that a community would elect someone who was not willing to fight for that group. It was the first real meritocracy where the right people ended up in the right positions and I would argue that it was this approach that really got us back on our feet.

When did "Royalism" end?

In a sense, it ended when the Royal Family handed over most of their roles to civilians. Some, of course, stayed on but that was because they were the best person for the job and not because they were a Royal, a meritocracy as I said. The two princes handed over their governorships to elected representatives some two years after the panic and although the Prince Regent remained in overall control of the day to day running of the country, he did appoint a Prime Minister and form a cabinet to replace the Royal Council. However, one can argue that "Royalism" as you call it, has never really ended. The King is the head of state in more than just name and all official organisations are Royal this or Royal that. If I were asked to define what Britain is I would have to say we are a "meritocratic representative monarchy" which I think makes us unique in the world and something to be proud of.

Militia

Ashwater, Devon

James Boardman is the Reeve for Ashwater and is responsible for the security of his local area, often based around a manor or settlement. His main role is to organise and train the local Militia and patrol for any remaining pockets of infected. I have joined him on a Wednesday, the traditional day for the Militia of Britain to train.

I guess the Militia was formed because the Army was just too small and overstretched to be able to guard every single settlement in the Safe Zones. I was moved to Ashwater from one of the camps during the resettlement program right before the harvest, I was a P3 you see, no useful skills. You have no idea how crushing it is to be told that. I was an insurance broker before The War and a bloody good one. I had a great job, a nice flat in Chelsea and had promotion prospects, going to the top my reports said. Ha if only I had started selling zombie insurance or Apocalypse protection I would have been laughing, as it was I was a P3 and a drain on the state. So they moved me somewhere I could do some good.

As a city boy, I had always thought that the countryside was a nice place to visit or go for the odd weekend shoot. Never realised just how much work there was involved in being a farmer. Christ, I learnt fast.

We were moved out by truck, about a hundred of us in a small convoy that stopped on the main road through the village and then we were allocated our houses. I was put into a beautiful thatched cottage, that would have been worth a fortune before the war, but was home to Mrs Janet Stallard, an elderly widow and owner of the cottage, myself and a family of four from Southampton. It was quite cosy but we actually got on really well. Mrs Stallard was a great host and knew everything about growing vegetables and storing the produce she grew.

Pretty much on the first day, we were put to work by the Village Rep. We used to call him The Chief. He was a sixty-year-old retired Army Officer with a chest load of medals and a moustache like a walrus. He may have looked like Captain Mainwaring from Dad's Army but he knew his stuff.

The first job was to build adequate defences for the village and this took the form of digging a bloody great ditch and mound around the entire place. I have never worked so hard in my entire life, it almost killed me. We were each given a five-meter stretch of ground and told to dig a ditch a meter deep and pile the spoil on the inside to make a wall. It took us a couple of days to finish and then another couple of days to finish tramping down the soil and cutting wooden stakes that went into the ditch. You can still see the wall over there.

He points to a low grass mount that runs around the village, it currently has sheep grazing on it.

It used to be a lot deeper and higher and quite a formidable defence.

Anyway, that was my first introduction to community spirit and civic duty and was certainly not my last. With the wall finished, we all slept a little safer at night, although the first time I stood guard was probably the most frightening experience of my life. Thank God we did it in pairs. Two to every ten meters of wall and jumping at every sound or movement. I don't know if you have ever stood guard at night but your eyes play tricks on you, you see things moving and your brain makes shapes out of shadows. A soldier once explained to me that it is because of the way the eye is built. During the day, the light comes into your eye and hits the receptors at the back of the eye and gives you an image but during the night the light gets picked up by receptors around the sides. That's why if you want to see something clearly at night you have to look to the side of it or move your eyes constantly. Anyway, none of us knew this at that time so we were twitchy as hell, every bush became a Ghoul and every breeze was a moan.

Where you ever attacked?

A few times yes, but we had a drill that when one section of the wall was attacked the reserve would deal with it and not those on the wall. We stayed where we were in case there were any more out there. It was pretty terrifying at first but then it became routine, it got to the point where we were down to one person every twenty meters and often not needing to call on the reserve for help. But that was months away and for the moment we were all still shit scared and still P3s but that was before the training teams and before the harvest.

Which came first?

The training. We were one of the first villages visited and it was incredible, to be given all this advice and skills, it made me feel useful again.

What did they teach you?

Well, there was a doctor who gave first aid lessons and some basic medical tips, like how to set a broken bone, cure fevers, that sort of thing. There was a gardener who started lessons but then took one look at Mrs Stallard's garden and promptly left for the next village. There was an electrician, a plumber and a builder who gave us lessons on how to maintain our appliances and keep the houses from falling down and there was the Army, four totally ordinary looking lads who put us through all kinds of hell for a week.

What did the training consist of?

Well, they kept it as simple as possible given that we were all civilians who, with the exception of The Chief, had never had anything to do with the military. They started by forming us up and putting us through some rudimentary drill movements, simple stuff like marching in step, turning on orders that sort of thing. I didn't understand why we were bothering with it but I later realised that the point of it wasn't to get us marching like Guardsmen on Trooping the Colour but to get us to react to orders. Anyway, we did a bit of that and then spent the rest of the time on weapon training and combat techniques all of which were pretty basic at this stage.

They took us through hand to hand combat tricks like how to get away from a G that has grabbed you, that sort of thing. They also told us the best way to kill them given the basic selection of weapons we had with us, mostly axes, bats, metal bars stuff like that.

The main thing they set up was a Command structure and the guard system. The first was quite easy to do. They set up these Command Tasks, you know the idea, get this barrel from A to B without touching C or D. It identified the leaders in the village and that was the start of our Militia units. The Chief was in charge, with four team leaders below him with about forty people in each team. The rota fell out from that. Each night one team would be on guard while another was the reserve and the rest slept. It was a good system as it meant that you did two nights on duty with two nights off. Once the attacks and sightings began to slack off we went down to a rota of only one team on a night, half on the wall, half on reserve. It was great, went up to three nights off and one on. We trained every Wednesday and everyone joined in. The only people who were exempt were the very young and the very old, although there weren't many of either in the first few years.

How often did you see someone from the Government?

Once the training team left we were pretty much on our own and it was only the truck drivers who came to collect the harvest that kept us appraised of what was going on outside our walls. It was only when the power came back on that we began to see people from outside the village, the first being the guy who came to install our village radio. That was the

121

end of our isolation really, I mean we had radios to listen to the Government messages but it was the first time we could broadcast out.

Things started to move pretty fast after that; the Regional Councils were set up and of course, the Chief was nominated as our rep and we received the first batch of cutlasses. It was beautiful, a truck turned up one day with a couple of grinning Gurkhas in the back and proceeded to hand out these fantastic tools. They gave us a twenty-minute master class before driving off to the next village still waving and smiling.

The next time that we saw the Government was when the recruiting teams came round, which must have been about a year into the Consolidation. They told us they needed strong men and women to help clear the country and I volunteered straight away, the village was too quiet for me I think. I had gotten a taste of action during the Panic and some of the skirmishes around the village but now I wanted to do more. I guess I had been bitten by the duty bug and wanted to do my bit to help save the country.

I left that afternoon and didn't come back until after VB day, that's when I took over as Reeve from the Chief, been doing it ever since and couldn't be happier. We still get the odd outbreak but to be honest, life is pretty quiet and I spend most of my time in my wood shop.

Settlement

Old Sarum Castle, Wiltshire

Sarum Castle rises above the ruins of Old Salisbury, an oval hill fort 400 meters long by 360 meters wide and over 150 meters high that has a long and illustrious history. It was first inhabited around 3000 BC by Stone Age Britons and continuously occupied through the Iron Age, where it was turned into a formidable hill fort with an outer and inner ditch. The Romans used it as a supply base before it was occupied as a royal castle of the Anglo-Saxon kings and later by William the Conqueror where he took the oaths of loyalty from his newly conquered kingdom. Sarum's decline began around 1220 AD with the construction of a new settlement at Salisbury and was eventually abandoned in the fifteenth century. During The War, the castle was occupied and defended by a group of refugees led by Mary Barker, who is now the Mayor of the rapidly growing settlement of New Sarum.

I first saw Sarum Castle when I was a little girl. It was a tourist attraction run by English Heritage back then and I remember being amazed at how deep the ditches were and how high the walls were. I guess that it was those memories that saved my life.

I started the Panic in Salisbury. I used to work behind the bar in one of the local pubs and when the Panic started I grabbed my family and friends and headed straight to the Cathedral. A lot of other people had the same idea I guess because the place was really crowded. Loads of people crammed into every knock and cranny and the priests trying to organise everyone and keep them calm. For the first few days, it was just chaos, lots of people either terrified and sitting quietly or frightened and talking really loudly. They were the worst, shouting and yelling, offering all sorts of useless advice that only really helped to get people annoyed. In the end, the Bishop had to get into the pulpit

123

and yell at people to calm down. He told us that there was plenty of food stockpiled, the cathedral had been sealed and we should just dig in and wait for rescue. He was right, people had brought lots of food with them, which the priests had collected and the Cathedral had been built during the Middle Ages when a church was a place of defence as well as a place of worship. All the windows were really high off the ground and the doors were solid oak and barricaded from the inside.

When did the first infected arrive?

It was non-stop really from the first days of the Panic. At first, they would turn up in ones or twos wandering out of the town and straight for the Cathedral, at the time I had no idea how they knew we were there, we were all told to keep quiet in the hope that they would not hear us, but they still found us. I guess it was smell or sound or something but they just kept coming. We didn't realise at the time but it was the moan that drew them to us. After the first one found us and just stood by the doors banging away and moaning more and more would arrive and moan and then more and more. Pretty soon we were surrounded by a horde of moaning ghouls scratching on the stone walls or banging on the doors. Thank God for the organist, he really kept us sane. I take it you were in the Safe Zones for most of the War?

I nod.

You're lucky then, you've never been under siege. It's not the fact that you have God knows how many infected outside trying to get in and eat you. I mean that's bad enough to fray your nerves but the bloody moaning, non-stop, day and night just drives you fucking mad. Have you ever heard a group of them together? It's like a low-pitched drone that you can feel in your chest, like those vuvuzelas from the South Africa World Cup. Anyway, the organist would play during the day and the choir would sing in the evening to try and distract people from the noise. Didn't work though, we had some people go mad and try and open the doors to escape, they spent most of the time tied up in a cellar or something, we never really asked.

When did you decide to leave?

It was only when our food stores started to run low that things got desperate. That was around late August and we had noticed that the weather was starting to turn; normally this time of year it was lovely and hot but this year it was cold and raining almost every day, on the plus side though at least we wouldn't die of thirst.

The first snows fell in the second week of September and just kept on falling and we all thought this is it, we would all freeze to death instead of being eaten. Not a bad way to go when you think about it.

It was only about a week later that we noticed that the moaning had stopped. It was a hell of a shock when we looked out from the stained-glass windows of the Cathedral and saw this snow-covered field with what looked like thousands of snowmen, none of us knew then that the infected froze in winter. There was much discussion about what we should do but eventually, it was decided that we should try and use this time to kill as many as possible before spring. We dismantled the barricades and opened the door, all of us ready to fight off a rush of Gs. Instead, we came face to face with a frozen body, arms raised in the act of banging on the door. I remember one man stepping forward and poking it with his crowbar and it just fell back into the G behind it. After that we were all like kids in a candy store, all that pent-up stress and strain just unleashed on these corpsesicles. We must have smashed the heads of hundreds of them in that first day alone.

It was that night that we had a group discussion about what we should do next, some argued for staying where we were, gathering supplies and digging in, others argued for leaving and trying to reach the Safe Zones. I was part of a small group who argued for trying to find somewhere more defensible and suggested Sarum Castle. In the end, we decided on all three options, one group gathered whatever supplies they could and set off for the Safe Zone, another decided to stay including all the priests and about sixty of us set off for Sarum.

It was a hell of a slog, all of us were carrying as much as we could and we headed into Salisbury. The whole place was covered in snow about two feet deep and we were all frozen within minutes, we had a quick chat and decided to hit the shops in the centre of town to try and find as many supplies as possible. I know what you're thinking, typical woman, end of the world and all she can think about is shopping. It was quite surreal really, sixty of us just wandering round Salisbury breaking into shops and stealing whatever we could.

I headed straight to the camping stores and found they had already been broken into but we cleared the place out. It was then that we made our most useful discovery; a bus. It was jackknifed across the high street with its doors open and we found the keys in the ignition, I guess that the driver must have abandoned it during the Panic. We turned it over and after a couple of tries and a lot of swearing, the thing started. It was fantastic, we put the heaters on full blast and began storing all our ill-gotten goods in the back. Driving it was a whole different matter though and it was bloody terrifying with the bus slipping and sliding on the snow, we went really slowly all the way to the castle.

It took about two hours to go two and a half miles, creeping along at a really slow speed. We would stop every time we passed a shop that we thought might have something useful. A group of us would get out and search the store for infected before we started to clear it out. Most of the time they were empty but every so often we would find one in a back room or trapped in a basement, we would have a brief fight on our hands and then we would take anything in the store that we thought would be useful. By the time we left town we had managed to accumulate quite a large haul of food, clothes, tools, tents, everything we thought would help us survive at Sarum. One of the most useful places we raided was the bookshop; DIY books, survival books, you name it, if we thought it could help, we took it. But on top of that, we had thousands of novels that would help keep people's minds busy and off their situation. We had built up quite a collection by the end of the war.

When we got to the castle I suggested that some of us should go and have a look first to make sure that it was all clear. A good lesson for life is never suggest anything unless you are prepared to do it yourself, that's how I found myself walking up the road to the entrance. Anyway, we stopped the bus right by the entrance and four of us got out and began walking up the road. It was quite hard going and we were all breathing really hard by the time we reached the outer wall. Six months of being cooped up in a cathedral with no exercise will do that to you. The outer wall was a huge mound of grass with a deep ditch behind it and then a really steep slope that led up to the bailey. The road cut straight through the outer wall and then onto a car parking area. We stopped here for a bit and waited to see if anything was moving or more importantly moaning but thankfully nothing.

We made for the keep which was another huge mound probably about one hundred meters around and accessible by a wooden bridge that crossed another ditch, only this time it was even deeper and steeper than the first. There was this makeshift barricade across the bridge that had collapsed in parts and slumped in front of it were the snow-covered bodies of a few Gs, their heads smashed in. We crossed the barricade very slowly, every sense alert for that tell-tale moan and got into the castle itself. Inside was worse than anything we had expected, there were bodies everywhere, some with heads caved in, some half-eaten; it was horrible and what was even worse was that everything was covered in snow making it look like something out of the Manson family's nativity scene. It was graveyard quiet and freaky but we could still see the potential for the place.

After that, we pretty much worked non-stop till spring. We cleared the keep of all the bodies and piled them in the car park, smashed all the heads to be extra sure and then set fire to them after soaking them in some diesel we drained from the bus. Took bloody ages and stank to high heaven but at least we knew that we wouldn't have to deal with disease on top of everything else. The next priority was getting some shelter set up and some sort of order to the keep. One of the guys in the group was a real outdoorsman and he took the lead on helping to set up the tents, a loo, a communal cooking area and all the details of camp life that you don't really think about. We dug out the old well for water and sent out foraging parties for wood, fuel, food and supplies. Thank God for the DIY stores in town, we absolutely cleared them out of everything we could fit in the bus; plastic sheeting and wood to help make shelters, tools, seeds to grow our own food, black bins to store food and more importantly water in, everything. I imagine it must have been the same for pretty much anyone else trapped in the Grey, button up in spring and then forage in winter.

By the time the snows started to melt we had built what resembled some sort of Mumbai slum inside a medieval castle. We had blocked off the two entrances to the bailey with barricades of cars and felled trees and had ripped up the bridge to make it impossible for the infected to get to us if they got inside the walls.

When did they start to reappear?

It was around late April, when the snow completely melted, that we started to see them, again I have no idea how they knew we were up there but they would make straight for us. Thankfully the hill was too steep for them to climb in most places and we had a bit of a laugh as they would try to scramble up at us only to fall back down. We found that they would follow us as we walked along the rampart and we used this to relieve the pressure on the main entrance when too many of them turned up. That first year was a bit touch and go and we had a number of them squeeze through the barricades but fortunately, they were dealt with by whoever was on guard.

What was life like for you in the castle?

It was very hard for the first couple of years, we didn't really know what we were doing you know. People died from the stupidest things, colds and infections mainly. We had food but didn't really know how to grow things properly and there was always the risk of a G coming over the walls. It was rare but it did happen, after the first few times we would shut ourselves up in the keep at night and only go out in pairs during the day. Having said that though, once we had been there for a while and things became routine, life actually became quite pleasant.

There was a rota for work which helped to give a bit of structure and everyone would help out, either tending the vegetable patch or helping out in the kitchen, although most of the time you just got in the way of John. He was our chef, a big blond guy who we nicknamed the Swedish Chef, you know the one from the Muppet show. Anyway, he was amazing and could produce fantastic stuff from really basic supplies; I can't tell you how much of a morale booster it was being able to eat decent hot food. We all spent time on guard as well, either patrolling the ramparts or manning the gate.

The second winter was like a pleasant break for us, no moaning and lighter guard duty but even then, the work didn't stop. We had decided that we needed a better wall at the main entrance and spent most of the winter building one from trees and barbed wire. We did the usual stuff as well, smashing heads, raiding the city and surrounding area but as the years went by we had to go further and further away to try and find supplies.

The one thing I always found funny was the way The War seemed to turn the world upside down and I don't just mean in the way that the modern world changed, it was in subtler ways. You know how winter used to be the time of rest and everything going into hibernation because of the cold? All that seemed to change around, at least it did in the Grey. As soon as the snows fell and the infected froze, that was when everything suddenly came to life. We would see birds, foxes, rabbits, all that life that had spent summer hiding suddenly came out. It was beautiful, like nature letting the Gs know that it was still there. Don't get me wrong it was no winter wonderland out there, in a lot of ways Darwinism had gone nuts.

What do you mean?

Well, I'm no expert by a long way but the entire food chain was turned on its head. The infected pretty much wiped out anything big and slow, so all cows, pigs and sheep were off the menu, save those in settlements, and everything else sort of went through some hyper-evolution to deal with the situation.

Can you give me an example?

Foxes! Bloody Foxes!

Before the war, anyone living in a city thought that they were a cute, little, ginger dog while anyone living in the countryside knew they were basically a great white shark with fur. Those little buggers became the wolves of the UK. They got bigger and meaner and in a lot of cases smarter. After the second winter, we used to have to stand guard at night to stop the bastards stealing all our food or livestock. They were worse than the packs of feral dogs or even the giant rats.

That was another problem. Rats had become the new staple diet of the food chain and because there was so much for them to eat in the first few years they got bigger and smarter and because of that, anything that wanted to eat them had to be big enough and smart enough to catch them. I guess that was why the dogs and cats got so big and mean.

I have a bit of a personal question if you don't mind? How did you all stay clean on the top of a hill?

We built a shower. We had raided a plumbing store and managed to put together a system that used an old boiler tank and copper piping. Basically, we would fill the boiler with rainwater then someone would have to turn a handle and pump the water around the system. The water would go through a coil of copper pipe that ran across the back of the cooking fire, warm it up and then out of a showerhead in a screened off area we had built. It was a bit of a gamble as it was either really hot or really cold but it kept us clean and when you got it right, oh there was nothing on earth like it.

When was your first contact with the Government?

It was some time in our third winter, we had been listening to the Government broadcasts on the radio of course but we had no way of answering back. I will quite happily say that the BBC saved our lives, the stuff that we learnt from the programmes was invaluable. Medical Hour taught us how to grow our own penicillin, Gardeners World taught me more than I ever thought possible about growing food but it was the comedies and news broadcasts that really gave us hope. You've got to remember that, for the first few years we had had no contact with anyone else and had no idea if there was a Government or even a country left. But listening to the radio and being able to hear about all the work being done in the Safe Zones and Burghs and every night being told by that wonderful posh British voice "Stay safe, stay alive. The Government is coming for you. Goodnight and good luck!" it made us see the light at the end of the tunnel.

The first proper contact was when we saw a helicopter in the distance flying north from the direction of Southampton, we screamed and shouted and waved which obviously had no effect. It was only when we remembered the bonfire ready to make potash for the veg garden that we got their attention. The helicopter came in and hovered over the castle before landing in the bailey. We all rushed over to see them and I remember feeling quite sorry for the pilots as they were bombarded with so many questions, they didn't know where to start and were looking quite flustered. I pushed to the front of the crowd and managed to shout everyone down before offering the pilots a drink. We all clustered around them as we walked up to the keep and sat in what we called the mess hall but was actually a rickety roof stretched between two of the castles old stone walls.

They explained that they were from the supply depot that was being built up in Southampton and were scouting for survivors so that they could get them back in touch with the Government. They stayed for about an hour and answered all our questions about what was going on around the country before they said they had to leave and report our location. Some people wanted to go with them but there wasn't enough room on the helicopter so we had to watch and wave them goodbye.

They were back a couple of hours later. This time they brought with them an old man and a load of poles slung under the helicopter. They dropped him off and he explained that he was a radio mechanic and was here to set up our system so we could talk to Southampton. It took an hour to set up the mast and wind turbine generators and then a couple of days for him to train some of us to operate it but we finally had a way of talking to the outside world. We got through to a kindly sounding old lady in Southampton who was the operator. I never got the chance to meet her but she had such a wonderful, well-spoken voice, really calm and poised which just relaxed you whenever you spoke to her, I guess that was why she got the job. Anyway, that first call lasted for a few hours and we told them everything we could think of about our situation. She asked us how many people we had, what food, water etc and did we need anything. By the end of the conversation, there was a shopping list a mile long and she promised something would be along soon.

"Something" turned out to be a bloody big helicopter, you know one of those ones with two rotas that landed in the bailey and just seemed to vomit people and supplies before taking off again. We all rushed over to greet these new arrivals who turned out to be the assessment team.

Assessment team?

Yeah, that was what they called themselves. Basically, the Government was too stretched to garrison every settlement they discovered so they would often send in a team of specialists to make them as defended and self-sufficient as possible. The assessment team was the first wave and were there to see what we needed and where they could help. They also brought a whole load of supplies with them to help brighten our day, things like blankets and chocolate and tea. God, I never realised how much I missed tea until then.

Anyway, these people had a good nosey around and worked out what we needed and fired off another shopping list. Within a day we had a carpenter and his tools to help build shelters and proper buildings, a doctor to set up a clinic, pigs, sheep, chickens and seed corn so we could plant wheat and make our own bread. It was amazing but more than all that was all the training we were given. There were a couple of soldiers who gave us recommendations on where to improve our defences, carpenters and doctors who gave lessons and then as quickly as they had arrived they were gone again on the helicopter to the next settlement.

After that, we were left pretty much to our own devices. We kept in contact with Southampton and when we needed supplies they would drop some off, if someone was really ill they would come in and pick them up but other than that we were left to get on with it.

Why do you think that was?

When they first turned up some people wanted to leave with them but the soldiers refused to let anyone on board; they said it was due to limited space in Southampton. What a load of bollocks. They wanted us there, safe and secure because it meant pinning down several thousand infected so they didn't have to deal with them. I can understand that and it was no big deal really, we were safe, pretty much impregnable and once we were given some cutlasses we could make a real dent in the swarm outside each winter. By the time we were liberated there were probably only about three thousand Gs left from the ten thousand that turned up in the second year.

How where you liberated?

Very slowly.

Seriously there was no huge battle and knights in shining armour rescuing the fair maiden in her castle. We were liberated by a bunch of combat engineers who were building the fortified motorway past our door. I found out later from a Major who was in charge of supply convoys that we were only chosen to be reconnected because we would make a good supply depot and there was an airfield just over the road. Always nice to be wanted!

Apparently, they started building the fortified motorways as soon as they had reoccupied the Western Docks in Southampton in order to reconnect the city airport with the dock and then they just spread out from there. They were already on their way to Salisbury when they found us and just decided to come straight here. Makes sense I guess but they took their bloody time, three months to go 25 miles.

We only realised what was happening when we saw this swarm of infected on the road into Salisbury banging on a shipping container that had been dropped across the road. At first, we had no idea what the hell was happening until the next morning when we saw this truck pick up the container and move it a few meters down the road. At the same time, two containers that had been pressed up against the sides of the first were pushed into place so that there was a U-shaped barrier across the road. Behind it, we could see a flurry of activity and then twenty minutes later the barrier moved again. We guessed they must have moved about five hundred meters a day and behind it, we could see those twelve-foot, rubble-filled bastion barriers that had been built on the pavement on either side of the road. It wasn't pretty but it was effective and we could see the infected wandering up and down the sides trying to get through. The whole road inside was a flurry of activity with lorries dropping off the pre-filled wall sections and tractors moving them into position behind the shipping containers.

It went on like this all day and all night for two days before they were building right up to our front door and pushing Gs out of the way with a bulldozer. It was a really happy moment when the final section went up. The big gate that we had built was pulled apart and we were finally reconnected to the outside world. We were still under siege from thousands of infected but we felt liberated.

Was that the end of The War for you?

God no, it was just the start. Our ramshackle little settlement was overnight turned into a bustling supply depot complete with bunkhouses for soldiers and engineers, grain silos and tall bastion walls. The settlement that we had set up pretty much died then and there as some people signed up for the Army and others just drifted off. Some of us stayed to help but mainly because this had become our home and we were loath to leave it. I volunteered to help organise the supplies and found myself in charge somehow and for four years we were the main stopping off point on the supply system. That was how New Sarum came to be; from a medieval castle to a supply depot to a growing town, makes me proud to think that I have helped to build something and leave a lasting legacy for future generations.

Authors note. A year after this interview a statue of Mary was erected in the market square of New Sarum. It was commissioned in secret by grateful citizens to honour the energy and passion of this incredible woman.

Islands

Brockhall Camp, Northamptonshire

General Palmerston and I have stopped overnight in the Army way station on the M1 near Daventry. The way stations evolved from the night camps built by the Royal Engineers and were originally intended as a secure location where the teams building the fortified motorways could rest. They evolved into base camps for the motorway patrol units, whose job it was to keep these vital routes clear. Today they serve much the same purpose but are no longer twenty miles apart; due to financial cuts and the reduced threat the distance between each camp is now sixty miles. We have just finished dinner with the officers of this camp and have retired to the mess ante-room to continue this interview.

When we sealed the Safe Zones my first thought was, thank God now we can take some of the pressure off and reorganise. How wrong I was. The hard work had really just started.

Why was that?

Well, for one thing, we still had the Northern and Sothern Zones to clear and at the same time, we had to guard the walls to prevent any breaches. To do all of these tasks we only had about a third of the Army scattered across both Safe Zones, the remainder were sealed up in their Burghs and fighting for survival. It was a hell of a situation and we needed to get a handle on it quickly.

The first step was to get the Safe Zones cleared but thankfully that process had begun as soon as the last section of the walls had been put in place. By the time the gates were sealed the Brigadier in charge of the "sanitation" was confident that he had destroyed most of the larger swarms and only smaller groups or individual zombies were still around. The second part was the guarding of the walls but again that was a fairly simple job as in those early days we did not have enough ammunition to allow the soldiers to take pot shots at the horde that was boiling and moaning at the base of the wall. All the lads could do was stand and make sure none formed a breach that would rip into the Safe Zone.

The biggest problem was the lack of men. As I said only a third of the Army was available in the Safe Zones and we were busy sanitising, guarding the wall or guarding the refugee camps. We were hugely overstretched and in danger of collapse. We were rescued, and I do mean rescued, by the Ministry of Resources. Thanks to McMillan and his frankly mad ideas we were able to empty the camps and give the military some breathing space to rest and reorganise. The best idea that man ever had was the concept of making each settlement as self-sufficient as possible and as far as CDS was concerned that meant in terms of military support too. That was where the Militia idea came in. The way we saw it, every single person who had made it to the Safe Zones had already proven themselves to be a survivor and should, therefore, be able to look after themselves. So we formed training teams and sent them out into the countryside to every farm, settlement and camp we knew of and trained an entire population how to fight. It wasn't pretty but it was functional and that was the watchword of the day. In those days if something could do the job then who cared what it looked like.

What can you tell me about the reorganisations?

That caused a lot of teddies to get thrown out of a lot of prams, the Navy and Air Force did not like having all their toys taken away. I mean what use is a Type 45 destroyer that is designed to combat air attacks against ground-hugging zombies or fighter jets for that matter. They just did not seem to get the concept that we were fighting a ground war now and all the equipment that we had built up for the last conflict was completely inappropriate. CDS was utterly ruthless, he told everyone who moaned about anything to either "shut up or get out".

We tied up most of the Royal Navy fleet leaving only the River class patrol boats and minehunters active, the rest was just too much of a drain on resources. Do you know how much fuel an aircraft carrier burned in a week, neither did I, but it was a hell of a lot. The nuclear subs were more useful as we could link them to the National Grid but the rest were tied up and left for most of The War with only enough maintenance to ensure that they were still seaworthy when the time came to use them again.

It was the same with the RAF, anything with a jet engine was grounded. We had Typhoons, Tornadoes, Harriers, C-17s all of it on airfields throughout the Safe Zones, the only things that were flying were the helicopters and the C-130s. The Army did not get off lightly either, all the tanks, armoured vehicles, artillery and attack helicopters were mothballed.

All of this left a lot of people suddenly out of a job and we essentially dragged them all kicking and screaming into the Army. We kept some of the Royal Navy crews on to take over some of the civilian ships and form the new Coastal Defence Force. Most of the pilots and ground crews were transferred onto the transport or helicopter fleet but the rest were drafted into either the Army or the Royal Marines. As you can imagine that required a lot of retraining. A lot of drill to get them to march together and a lot of marksmanship practice to teach them to shoot straight. Although it wasn't until we were able to get some munitions factories going that we could really turn up the training. Eventually after a lot of blood, sweat and tears, not to mention a lot of swearing we had something that resembled an army.

What can you tell me about Ireland?

If you know anything about British and especially English history you would know that there is a long history of involvement in Ireland, most of it aggressive, that goes all the way back to William the Conqueror. Northern Ireland was still part of the UK and we had maintained a large military presence there despite the success of the peace process and when the Panic hit the Army essentially got as many people as they could into their camps and Burghs and then sealed the gates. Fortunately, Northern Ireland had a very small population, something like 2 million and most of that was centred around the cities which were where our Burghs where. The result of all this was that within a year of the Panic, the Brigade in Northern Ireland had pretty much cleared the cities of infected, an incredible feat I think you will agree. Of course, there were still a few knocking around here and there and of course, there were still those that were wandering over the border.

The Republic of Ireland was a whole different issue though; a small population and an even smaller Defence Force, some 10,000 strong. By the time the Panic really hit, with most of the Garda already dead and their military struggling to cope, their Government collapsed and fled to Galway. It was at that point that they made a formal request for military aid from the British Government and although that sounds like a very simple request it was hugely emotive.

Ireland is England's original sin in the same way that the US treatment of the Native Americans and the Australian treatment of the Aborigines is theirs. To the Irish, we represented a thousand years of intervention, invasion and conquest and now we were planning to send an army to help them out. The negotiations began in late September of that first winter and as you can imagine there was a lot of political wrangling involved. By the end of the first week, it was pretty clear that the negotiations were hung up on the terms of the agreement, understandably the Irish were a little worried that we were going to annex them. It was only when one of the Government negotiators suggested that Ireland formally request to join the Commonwealth and then request a military alliance that the deadlock was broken and we had our agreement.

Could you explain the terms of the agreement?

Well, essentially it required the UK to provide military support to aid the Armed Forces of the Republic of Ireland and support their Government in reclaiming their country. In practice, it meant a lot of sleepless nights for me as we planned the first major operation of the war.

Sorting out the supply issues alone almost broke me as we were planning an expeditionary operation to recapture a country at a time when the UK's economy was in ruins and we barely had enough ammo and equipment to cope. I was repeatedly asked by my staff why we were doing this at such a breakneck speed, why not wait until all the fledgeling industries were up and running before we attempted to clear Ireland? My answer was always the same; because a friend is in need and they have asked us for help.

There were, of course, greater political motives and I think a lot of credit can be given to the Prince Regent for taking the long view. By that I mean he was looking both at the short term; gain the trust of the Irish and atone for the sins of our ancestors and at the same time open up Ireland as a place of refuge to people across Europe. While in the long term he knew that by accepting Ireland into the Commonwealth and helping them it would sow the seeds for future operations to help Commonwealth countries and build a stronger organisation that could help to rid the world of the infected threat.

By the time spring came around we had managed to scrape together some ten thousand soldiers, trained them and equipped them with whatever we had available. At first glance, though they appeared to be less of an army and more of a mob. From the look of them, you would have thought that a bunch of Orcs had fallen off the pages of Lord of the Rings. All of them were in mismatched clothes; a mixture of old uniforms, looted hiking gear and lots of different types of headwear. The one thing we made sure each man had was a good set of boots as he was bloody well going to need them. Everyone had a rifle and as much ammunition as they could carry but after that, each soldier carried whatever close combat weapon they could find, anything from crowbars and meat cleavers to wood axes and metal bars. If it could crack a skull it was carried. I remember this one chap, big Scottish lad, had found a bloody great claymore from somewhere and had it strapped to his back like an extra from Braveheart, very odd but apparently, he was lethal with it.

We mustered them all at Garelockhead and began shipping them over to Belfast in February, the crossing was bloody awful and I can say that from personal experience as I went over to take personal command of the whole thing. I guess that it must have been something to do with the colder temperatures that the entire world was experiencing but the seas were rough and choppy and no matter how plush a cruise ship you commandeer, seasickness is not pleasant.

By mid-February, we had managed to get the entire army and it supplies across, formed it up in the cleared Belfast harbour and linked up with the Brigade garrisoned there.

What was your plan for the clearance?

With only 15,000 troops to work with, I was rather limited in my options, there was no way that we could use the American approach. We just did not have the numbers to line them up and march across the whole country so I decided to use the same approach that we had used at Junction. Before you say it, I know that everyone at Junction died but the plan itself was sound; it only failed because of the numbers. At Junction a single Battalion took on one and a half million infected, that was odds of three thousand to one and that is why they were overrun. My plan was to even out the numbers, disperse the Battalions across the countryside, advance on numerous different routes and take on smaller numbers of infected on ground that favoured us.

However, before any of that could happen we had to ensure our rear was secure and here the weather was a blessing. It may have been bloody cold and hard work wading through the snow to smash any infected we could find but it made me, and I hope the rest of the army, happy that we would not have an outbreak in the rear areas.

By mid-March, the weather was starting to warm up and it was time to send out the Battalions to their start points. My plan here was that each unit would take a main road and march down it making as much noise as possible. Whenever they encounter a single infected, or group of infected an appropriate number of soldiers would stop to take it down. Whenever they met a group that needed a larger response the unit would find a defensible location, like a hilltop, and then let the infected come to them. In this way, we managed to cover a huge amount of land in quite a short amount of time and while it was not perfect it did manage to clear most of the country.

Obviously, we had to change tactics when it came to cities as these tended to have the largest swarms surrounding the small groups of survivors. In this case, the unit would stop outside the city and dig a marching camp similar to the Roman Legion camps of old. Once this was done the unit would bang away and make as much noise as possible in order to draw as many of the infected out of the city as possible. In reality, all it took was one of them to see you and moan and that moan then carried to others who then moaned and homed in on the first one and so on and so on until you had an entire horde pouring down on you. I was with the 1st Battalion Irish Guards outside Dublin with half the city bearing down on us, pipes playing and drums beating in the background and those wonderful soldiers firing like clockwork as row after row of infected were taken down. Of course, the hard part came when we had to clear through the cities for those that were trapped and could not get to us.

It took five months but by the time the first snows fell in September I was shaking hands with the Irish Premier in Galway. It was a hell of a moment and at the time I had no idea how important Ireland would become.

How do you mean?

142

Well for one it was a huge moral and strategic victory. We had proven to the world but more importantly to ourselves that we were not beaten and that we could fight back. I think it really helped to show people the light at the end of the tunnel to keep going and to keep fighting. At the tactical level, we had tested many different techniques in "zombie warfare", discarded those that did not work and refined those that did, in many ways Ireland was a trial run for everything that came after.

At a political level, it had shown leadership from the UK Government, something that was badly needed after that farce in Stirling. It drew us closer together with Ireland and would eventually lead to them being a founding member of the New Commonwealth.

Economically it opened up huge areas of Ireland to farming and within two years the Ministry of Resources had built up enough infrastructure for Ireland to become the breadbasket of Britain and then eventually Europe.

But most important was the fact that we could open up Ireland to all those refugees still floating around the world's oceans. The surprising part was how few refugees actually turned up, barring, of course, the Pope who arrived with half the Vatican in tow. I think the reason for this was that during the Panic, most European refugees had headed for Iceland in the mistaken belief that it was cold all year round and would be safe from the infected. You just have to look at it now to see how wrong they were. Still, it allowed the UK to offer sanctuary to those who could make it. Like I said earlier, the Prince Regent had taken the long view and it had paid off.

What about the operation in Cyprus?

Well, that was a whole different kettle of fish. That operation had nothing to do with the UK Government but was a brilliant example of a local commander taking the initiative and reacting to the situation on the ground. Something that was very rare in the pre-war years, not because of the commanders you understand but because Whitehall and the MOD insisted on running every war from London. The soldiers called it "the long screwdriver".

So what was the situation on the ground?

Well in the pre-war years, Cyprus was still split between the Turks controlling the north of the island and the Greeks controlling the south. The UN force kept the peace between them and two battalions provided security for the UK Sovereign Base Areas at Akrotiri and Dhekelia. We had something like 3,500 troops on the island as well as a large contingent of civilians, families and Cypriots who lived and worked in the camps.

When we implemented Op Senlac the Commander British Forces Cyprus was ordered to seal his gates and dig in for a long-term siege. Have you read his book? You should, it is a bloody good read. It was absolutely astounding what they went through in the first year alone. No sooner had they finished their defences and sealed the gates, then the first outbreaks began to occur on the island. Initially the infected were dealt with quickly by the large military presence on both sides of the divide but as the outbreaks got worse and more and more refugees from the Middle East began to arrive, the situation deteriorated rapidly. The problem was that with our troops pulled back behind their walls there was no one to stop the Greeks and Turks from facing each other down across the dividing line. The bloody fools were so concerned that the other side was going to make a land grab that they kept most of their troops on the line while the Island descended into chaos behind them. Eventually the inevitable happened and someone took a shot at someone else and all hell broke out. Within minutes there was a full-scale conventional war raging across the length of the Island with tanks and artillery being used on population centres. It was insanity, two sides lashing out at each other with no clear objectives, just years of fear and mistrust culminating in a stupid bloody fight. For two weeks both sides battered each other to a stalemate, wrecking

God knows how much of the island in the process and killing God knows how many civilians.

It was at that point that the British commander decided that enough was enough and began his break out from the base areas. His plan was to push out across the Island, eliminate any infected that he came across and link up with any surviving soldiers or civilians. As I understand it he had a relatively easy time of it as the vast majority of the infected on the island had been drawn to the dividing line by the noise of all the fighting. He used this breathing space to get as many civilians back into the base areas as possible before he swept from one side of the island to the other. Within three months he had swept the island clear of infected, rescued most of the civilians and managed to knock some sense into what was left of the Greek and Turkish militaries and got them to work together. It was an incredible achievement and he deserved every single one of the honours and awards he was given.

By the end of the operation, there was a stable and secure island in the sea of chaos that was the Middle East, that was able to act as a staging point for the later UN operations. In the short term though, we were able to use the huge radio transmitters and receivers that were on the island to broadcast the BBC World Service to anyone still alive. I think that ability to reach all those people in the Middle East, North Africa and Europe and provide them with useful information and advice but most of all hope, was one of the most important things that Britain ever did in The War.

Supply lines

Exeter

It is early morning in Exeter and Josh Peck has kindly offered to take me on one of his daily patrols. Today's route is up the coast to Southampton where he will take the time to show me the former supply dock which played such a huge role in The War **effort. We take a slow twenty-minute flight following the coastline. Josh is flying the helicopter while I have taken the role of observer. Normally Josh would be accompanied by a qualified spotter whose job it was to monitor the towed sonar. This system is used in conjunction with a line of sonar buoys placed around the entire coast to give some warning of a seaborne incursion. With several million infected still roaming the sea floor, this is still a very real threat.**

You know, if you had flown this route before The War you just wouldn't recognise it today. I mean look at it, the entire coastline is essentially one long shingle beach, great during those long summer months for family trips but bloody awful when it came to defence, you can see why they drew the defensive line at Exeter. All those lovely seaside towns are still empty today, people just don't want to live near the coast anymore and they definitely don't go to the beach anymore. It's such a shame; I have some fond memories of family beach holidays from around here.

Anyway, I told you how I was recruited right, because of my flying skills, well I tell you those skills were nothing compared to what I had to learn when flying for the military. I thought I knew how to fly but some of the things they taught me to do and then I did myself later, I never thought you could do with a helicopter. All my training was going on at the same time as the reforms in the military, you know all that stuff about laying up the big navy ships, reorganising the Army and grounding anything the RAF flew that couldn't carry supplies. I heard a lot about it in the bar. A lot of bitching and moaning about how the Government were getting rid of their fancy fighters. I just couldn't see the problem though, maybe because I was a Civi but what use is a fighter jet against infected. The way I heard it, the Government had spent billions on jets designed for the Cold War that were obsolete when they finally arrived, so was it any surprise that they were all grounded. There was a lot of rivalry between the helicopter pilots and the fast jet boys and God did we have a laugh when all those arrogant buggers ended up flying the transport fleet, it must have been like going from driving a Ferrari to a milk float.

Part of the reform was all the Army, Navy and RAF helicopters being grouped together under the control of Helicopter Command. Back then the main aim of the unit was the resupply of the Burghs. Most of them were inland and therefore not accessible from the sea. None of them were big enough for the C-130s so it was up to Heli Command to get what we could to them. One of my first missions was flying a doctor and some supplies to one of the Burghs near Glastonbury. It was a bit hairy as I was in quite a big Heli, one of the Merlins, and it was a very tight landing zone. I almost clipped the outer wall at one point but just managed to put her down in one piece, still brings me out in a cold sweat how close that one was.

Those flights became fairly routine after a while and it was because of the regular flights that we discovered a lot of the un-registered settlements. No one had any idea how many people were living in The Gray or where but it was because of flights like mine that people were rediscovered. One time I was on a routine resupply run and was flying over Poole when my door gunner caught sight of this group of people waving madly from the roof of a block of flats, I circled around and hovered over the roof trying to find somewhere to land but it was way too small. So I got my co-pilot to write a note saying we would be back with help, we stuck it in an empty water bottle and dropped it onto the roof. We hung around long enough to make sure they got it, marked the location on our map and carried on with our mission. When we got back to base we informed the higher ups and asked for permission to drop them some supplies but we were denied.

Did they say why?

Nope. That's the great thing about the military they don't have to explain themselves. I did find out though, by talking to some people who worked in the HQ, that there weren't enough resources available to resupply these settlements and the plan was to record their locations as we discovered them and then move on. Apparently, the RAF were already using their UAVs to scan the country trying to track the swarms and had stumbled across a number of settlements. They started to use the swarms to find the settlements; the theory was that you looked for the big swarms and it would be a fair bet that there would be people alive right in the centre of it.

We went on like this for about six months and it was fucking awful. Every time we flew a resupply run, we would fly over or near a settlement that was under siege and see these people looking up at us or standing with arms raised like they were begging me for help.

Did you ever try to help?

No, no I didn't, I was never that brave. I heard a story though about this one Chinook pilot who rescued a load of people from a block of flats that was in the process of being overrun. The story goes that he was flying past and saw people crammed onto the roof, trying to keep the access door closed. Apparently, he asked for permission to rescue them, was denied by Command but just said fuck it and went in anyway. He dropped the rear ramp and backed that massive helicopter onto the roof just as the access door was broken open. He saved sixty people that day, he was a hero but when he got back to base he was arrested and put in the stocks in the centre of Exeter. Now normally people in the stocks got pelted but word had got around about what he had done and he wasn't touched. People would feed him, bring him water and sit with him to pass the time. Pretty soon Command realised that they had made him a hero and let him out. I heard the BBC did a programme on him, he was a brave guy and he changed everything.

How?

Well, Command very rapidly realised that unless they changed their policy the settlements would fall and the Safe Zones would be inundated with infected from the Grey who would have been kept busy elsewhere. That was when we began to fly resupply missions to the settlements. At first, it wasn't very much; some bread, salt, seeds anything that we could spare. But as the Safe Zones got back on their feet and the Ministry of Resources got its act together we began to fly out more and more supplies as well as advisory teams.

That was a tough job. Sometimes it was easy, fly in, do the inspection and then fly out but sometimes the teams went in for the long haul. Some of the settlements were impossible to land in so supplies were dropped in off the back of the Heli. There were a couple of times when the advisory teams had to fast rope in knowing that they would be there until they were liberated. Balls of steel some of them!

So it was essentially self-preservation that motivated the supply drops?

Well yes and no. I can't talk for the higher-ups but you can see their reasoning. Every infected out there was better than one knocking on the door of the Safe Zones. It may be cold but it bought the rest of us time to get prepared and to go back on the offensive. At least we knew where most of them were and that every winter the people in the settlements would be killing off more and more of them just like we did on the Safe Zone walls.

Look, we're here.

Josh nudges me as we begin our flight up the Solent and into the mouth of the Estuary. Even though ten years have passed since the end of The War the city is still a remnant of its former self. The massive wartime fortifications centre on the dockyards with the outer wall encircling the area within the A35. It is an impressive sight, made even more so by the fact that most of this work was undertaken at a time when Britain was on its knees.

Can you tell me about the operation to recapture this place?

Sure. As I understand it the big idea was to create a defended supply depot that would act as a resupply point once we began to take back the country. The whole fortified motorway thing came a bit later when command realised the value of reconnecting the Burghs. The plan was to amass a fleet of container ships off the coast of the Isle of Wight with all the supplies that we would need for the op. From what I heard from the Navy boys that took quite some doing as a lot of those ships were either floating refugee camps or infested with Gs. I can't imagine what it must have been like for the Royal Marines having to clear those hulks.

Anyway, they eventually got enough of a Merchant Navy back together to ferry all the supplies from Plymouth to the holding point and then they waited for a week while a destroyer sat in the mouth of the Estuary and banged away with its active sonar. It was a bit of an experiment, but the scientists who had been studying the infected guessed that the sound of the ping would attract a lot of the ones that were wandering around the sea floor or under the docks and draw them away from the landing site. Apparently, it worked really well, as within a few days there was a hell of a crowd under the ship, of course, that still left the problem of what to do with all those bastards. Then someone came up with the idea of dropping a depth charge on top of them. I hear they rigged one up with a noisemaker and dropped it right in the middle of the crowd before steaming off at full pelt. A mate of mine was flying overhead at the time and he says that he could see this shock wave ripple through the water and then this massive plume erupted into the air. It must have worked like a dream as they are still using the technique today, "Ping and drop" it's called.

At the same time as all that was going on the pilots were getting our orders and briefings. The plan was that we would fly to Cowes on the Isle of Wight, collect our chalk of soldiers and then "Air Assault" them onto the Eastern Docks at the same time as the first cargo ships docked.

It was so exciting, the first proper military thing we had really gotten to do as none of us in Southern Command were involved in the Clearance of Ireland or Op Euston. More importantly, for everyone was that it finally felt like we were starting to take back our land, it was a hell of a rush and more than one person overreacted, me included. **Op Euston was the operation to move the Northern Defensive Line to a new position along the A69. It was undertaken in the depth of winter to limit zombie attacks with the aim of reclaiming the cattle and sheep pasture lands of Northumberland which would be needed for the coming Restoration.**

As we were lifting off from Cowes and getting into formation to fly down the Solent some funny bugger started to hum the Wagner song from Apocalypse Now on the net and pretty soon we were all humming along with big grins on our faces and all the soldiers in the back joining in. It got a bit silly after that as helicopters started to weave and dodge as if they were assaulting a defended beachhead. Eventually someone got on the net and told us to stop "fucking around" and we did, right up until the last moment when we came into land and almost every pilot slammed their bird in like it was a proper combat drop and then pulled hard in the take-off, trying to evade all those zombie Anti-Aircraft guns. Still, it got the job done and we put over three hundred soldiers onto the docks in ten minutes just as the ships started to dock and the first tractors rolled off.

It was one hell of a sight. I was ordered to stay on station with a Quick Reaction Force of thirty soldiers so I had a bird's eye view of the proceedings. The soldiers all spread out and began to sweep the dock of Gs before they formed a perimeter along the outside of the main car park, it took them a long time as the place was a fucking mess. I guess that during the Panic people must have just dumped their cars and run for whichever boat was available. There was scattered luggage, crashed cars and here and there rotting corpses but strangely very few infected. Part of this was probably due to it being late August and it was starting to get colder but I think that it was because they had already killed everything in the city and then buggered off to find something else to eat.

At the same time, the ships were unloading armoured tractors that set to work on the cars and I do mean set to work. They slammed them into piles with bulldozers, piled them ontop of each other to form barricades or just pushed them into the estuary when they ran out of space. Within an hour they had cleared a space for all the supplies to be unloaded, about an hour after that they began building the perimeter wall along the main road using pre-cast concrete wall sections. It was like looking down on an ant's nest, there was just so much activity all going on at the same time. It should have been chaos but somehow everything seemed to work together.

By the time it got dark they had built the wall and sealed off the peninsula that the docks sit on and I was ordered to land and shut down for the night but to stay near my helicopter in case we were needed. It is embarrassing to say it now but I was having so much fun. I know that doesn't seem right given how many people died in the Panic and then the Restoration, we are supposed to be all solemn and stoic about it, but I was having the time of my life. I had taken part in an air assault and my first major operation and I felt like a soldier like I was doing something that mattered. I know that the supply runs were essential but it didn't feel like I was taking the fight to the enemy. Before this Op, we had just been surviving and now we were attacking. I think that helped to keep people going.

Anyway; it was a really quiet night with no attacks on the perimeter and it pretty much stayed that way for about a week, by then the wall was damn near impregnable and we were starting to push out to the airport. My flight had been ordered to stay on and provide a combination of heavy lift and scouting so were working flat out 24 hours a day. I tell you, I have seen some things in my time but one of the most impressive was how fast those docks came to life. Within a week the walls had been built and a fully working base set up, two weeks after that we had built a fortified route to the airport and secured it for the heavy-lift aircraft to come in. After that, things just grew and grew, I got rotated out for a few weeks back to Exeter to refit and by the time I flew back the place was twice the size. They had cleared the West Quay and there was an almost constant stream of ships unloading stores, there was an entire section set up for the recycling of anything that could be scavenged from the thousands of containers on the dock and from the city. An entire warehouse district had been converted into a hydroponics farm and another area had been converted into a biofuel farm, it was staggering. What I found really reassuring was when one of my fight crew said that "If we can do all this for a supply depot then the Gs 'll be shitting themselves when we properly get going".

RESTORATION

Prepare to Move

Ministry of Defence, London

It has taken two days for General Palmerston and I to reach London following his inspection tour of Militia and Army units en route. With the old Ministry of Defence building destroyed in the Great Fire, it was decided that it would be more cost effective to repair, restore and modernise Horse Guards, the Old Admiralty building and Admiralty Arch, all of which had survived the fire reasonably well. Having finally completed the work we are now ensconced in the office of the Chief of the Defence Staff on the first floor of Horse Guards, the former office of the Duke of Wellington. The office itself is beautiful with wide open windows that overlook St James Park and a subtle green colour scheme that seems to draw the parkland into the office. General Palmerston is sitting behind the desk of the Duke of Wellington that miraculously survived the fire.

They call it the Restoration now but at the time all I could call it was a bloody great mistake. It was in May, a few weeks after Op Euston, when Sir Richard told us the good news. He had just come back from a meeting with the Prince Regent and the Royal Council and he gathered all the senior staff together and told us that the decision had been made to go on the offensive and reclaim our country.

What was the reaction?

I was bloody stunned and so were a lot of the other officers in the room. There was a moment of silence before everyone started blurting out questions. It took Sir Richard three attempts to quiet the room before he had to resort to slamming his cane on the table and yelling for silence. "The order has been given and we will carry it out to the best of our ability" and that was that.

Why did the decision cause such distress?

I wouldn't say that distress is the right word; surprise and concern but not distress.

Why the concern then?

Well, the majority of the senior staff didn't think the country was anywhere near ready to support such a massive operation. The orders called for a spring offensive which only gave us ten months to get everything in place and that was nowhere near enough time. We had soldiers to train, equipment to manufacture and God knows how many bullets we would need to produce. Most armchair generals who think they know something about waging war believe that it is all about putting troops in the field to defeat the enemy. Anyone with half a brain will tell you that it is all about logistics; the ability to keep your men feed, armed and warm. It is not cool and it is not sexy but it is absolutely vital. In World War II it required the mass industrialisation of Great Britain and the US to defeat the Nazis but here we were with a country that was only just beginning to get back on its feet, a limited industrial capability and no prospect of support from our allies.

On top of all that, we were facing a deadly and determined enemy that would need to be cleared from every inch of land, had no concept of fear and could not be starved or beaten into submission. We had to be thorough in our work since it would only take one infected to start the whole cycle again.

Let me tell you a little secret about how you win a war. In every single conflict, that man has ever fought in the objective has never been to totally destroy your enemy. The trick is to apply enough force to make the enemy roll over and surrender. It is a tried and tested formula that has work for every battle in history; Cannae, Hastings, Normandy.

But that approach doesn't work against the infected; they have no fear, no moral component; there is no civilian population to protest The War and make a government change their policy. They cannot be demoralised, bribed or reasoned with, every single one of them is a self-contained war machine whose sole purpose is to kill and devour us. All this meant that everything I had ever learnt about offensive military action was now obsolete. That was the situation facing us when the decision was made and that was what concerned me.

Did you raise your concerns?

Right after Sir Richard had made the announcement, I walked into his office and told him that I thought this was a mistake, that we were not ready, there was no plan, there were not enough bullets; anything I could think of to try and dissuade him from what I thought was a suicidal course of action.

Of course, he was ready for me and very calmly asked if I thought that he had not raised every single one of those points with the Prince? He sat me down and very gently explained that whether we were ready or not the country needed to attack.

What did he mean by that?

You remember the situation back in the spring of the third year, how things were starting to look up? For the first time, we had a surplus of food, our industrial base was just beginning to swing into full production, the operation in Ireland has been a success and we had just moved the Northern Defensive Line. To many people, it looked like we were starting to take the first steps on the road to recovery and that was having a tangible effect on the population of the Safe Zones; suicide rates were down, as were the overall death rates. People seemed to be genuinely much happier.

Imagine what would have happened to that if we had decided to just sit behind our walls and wait for the infected to rot away, you could already see it happening to some of the very early ones. It would have had a devastating effect on morale not to mention the national psyche. Don't forget that in the British mind we were still the country that had won an empire, defeated fascism and endured the Blitz. As a people, we had survived all that and still been able to hold our heads up and say that we fought for every second of every day. "Blitz Mentality" it was known as, I called it British bloody-mindedness.

Now imagine that we had just hunkered down and left all those people in the Grey to their fate; how would we be able to look ourselves in the mirror, more importantly, how would we be able to look our children in the eye ever again?

No, the Prince was right. We needed to go on the offensive and we needed to win.

What was the military situation at that time?

Let me show you.

General Richard produces a worn map of the British Isles and spreads it on the desk.

The red areas represent territory under our control, so Ireland, everything north of Newcastle and Carlisle and everything west of Exeter. These little red dots scattered across the country are the Burghs and all the settlements that we have been able to locate and resupply. Everything else is the Grey, infected territory and generally hostile to us.

From a military point of view, we were actually very secure. We were safe behind our high walls, our casualties had been surprisingly light in the past year and we were beginning the process of training the next generation of soldiers. We could have quite happily sat back and conducted our winter sweeps along the front of the walls and let the infected rot. It would not have been grand or courageous but it would have saved lives and cost us very little. However, that all changed when we went on a war footing. We had to ramp up the training and change it from defensive to offensive tactics, it also meant a huge amount of reequipping needed to be done.

Where we were really lacking was in the industrial capacity to support the army. We had only just managed to recapture the munitions plant just outside Newcastle and were in the process of getting that set up to churn out as many bullets as possible.

The final point was that we did not have enough bastion walls, we had used them when we built the Safe Zone walls and then later to move the Northern Line but as the plan for the Restoration took shape we realised that we would need an unprecedented amount of these things. Again the Ministry of Resources came to our aid and simply turned every spare person they could find to the task of manufacturing them. It was a Herculean effort and those workers deserve as much credit for victory as the soldiers.

When it came to how we were going to actually clear the country we realised pretty early on that we couldn't just march south in a straight line and sweep it clear as the Americans did. The country was too bloody big and we did not have enough men. On top of that, we were up against a hell of a lot of infected and if we took them all on at once then we would be overrun and slaughtered.

We had estimated that with something like 15 million people in the Safe Zones, Ireland and the Burghs and another 15 million dead or reanimated in the Great Panic that left somewhere in the region of 45 million zombies, give or take the few million that we had killed already. What we needed to do was divide them into manageable chunks and take them on at a slow measured pace. That was the basic outline of the plan but what we really needed to do was test the low-level tactics and check if the whole thing was even feasible and that is where Carlisle came in.

Battle of Carlisle

Port Stanley, Falkland Islands

Jock MacTavish has just returned from one of his frequent patrols around the fortified settlement of Stanley. Though there is very little risk of zombie attacks in this bleak corner of the world, mainly due to the cold weather and icy seas, there is still a risk from pirates who frequently raid the island for supplies including the large sheep population. We have just finished dinner and while his wife and children clear the dishes we sit at the table to talk.

I know it sounds strange but you know what I felt when we got the orders that we were going over the wall? Relief! Weird isn't it but I guess I was just really glad to be finally taking the fight to the enemy. Sure I had taken part in the clearance of the Safe Zone and spent my time on the wall like everyone else. I had missed out on Ireland and Euston as I was helping to train the Militia so I was pissed off about that but this was different; it was the first chance to have a go at the G's in their back yard. To give them a fucking good kicking and say that we weren't going to roll over and die.

Don't get me wrong though, I was still shitting myself as we were preparing for the Op. Command pulled together a mixed bag of soldiers drawn from every Regiment in the army, it was really clever when you think about it. If the Op goes badly then only a platoon from each Regiment is lost but if it goes well, then that platoon goes back to their unit and starts bragging and spreading the good news, everyone starts to feel more confident. Genius really!

Anyway, they pulled this force together, something like nine hundred men with another hundred support troops to make it a nice even thousand and billeted us in Fort Rockcliffe at the western end of the wall and began training us together as a Unit. Don't get me wrong, we had been training ever since the end of the Op in Ireland on the new tactics that had been tested out there but this was different. We were drilled remorselessly until we could move together and given more ammunition to play with than most of us had ever seen before.

Could you describe the training that the rest of the army received?

After Ireland, the Army conducted a review of all the engagements and all the different tactics that had been tried; discarded those that didn't work and used those that did. In the end, they worked out that there were two things that were essential to defeating the Gs; marksmanship and psychology. Typical of the bloody Army that it takes them six months to work out what I could have told you in a minute. Marksmanship was obvious, you want to kill a G you have to destroy the brain but hitting a target that small, while it's moving, requires some fucking good shooting. The pre-war army trained us to shoot at the chest because it is a nice big easy target and would put a human down in one shot. You shoot a G in the chest it will just knock it on its arse or worse you break its spine.

Why is that worse, surely disabling it is a good thing?

If you break a G's back or blow off a leg, then it becomes a crawler and they're fucking dangerous. Ideally, you want your G standing up where you can see him so you can get a nice clean shot. Crawlers are like fucking land mines, you can't see them until you step on one and then they take your leg off. Happened to a mate of mine during one of the clearance sweeps. We were patrolling through the Highlands and all of a sudden, he screamed and disappeared into the tall grass, we rushed over and this G had grabbed him and was chewing on his leg, we hadn't heard the fucking thing because its throat had been ripped out sometime in the past. It was bloody horrible, we had to put them both down, none of those nice euthanasia jabs that came along later, but we learnt the lesson the hard way and we always brought dogs with us after that. Saved a lot of lives those lovely furry bastards, they always found the crawlers before we did.

The shooting training was just never-ending, every day we were on the ranges firing at these wooden targets fixed to a conveyor belt that was meant to simulate the Gs getting closer and closer. After Junction and a load of other battles the Army had worked out that if you slowed the rate of fire right down you could hold off Christ knows how many Gs as long as you had enough ammunition and enough men to fire it. So we practised day after day with a big bass drum thumping out a beat every second and on every beat, we would fire.

The other part of the training was the psychological conditioning. One of the things that made the Gs so deadly wasn't their bite or their determination, it was the fear that they generate. The irrational panic that drove people to do stupid things and act even more stupidly, just look at all the crap that happened during the Panic, here and around the world. All that caused by the fear that these things caused.

Command's bright idea was to take away that fear, by making us rationalise the G, to understand it. We learnt all about what they can and can't do, their methods of attack, that sort of thing. As I said we had all spent time on the walls practising our shooting and that really helped. Fact is that when you come down to it, a G is just a slow-moving, shambling hunk of meat and as long as you keep calm and keep some space between you and it, you'll be fine.

All that was well and good but you try telling that to me as we were on the boats crossing the river. I was shitting myself, every thought in my head was screaming at me that this was a stupid idea, this was their territory now and that we were all going to die but I was a Sergeant now and I had a responsibility to my men. I looked around at those lads and lasses in my platoon, seeing how they were all looking at me and my Platoon Commander, trusting us to get them through this; all that fear just fell away and I promised myself that we would all get through this in one piece.

It was April the fucking first, can you believe that; some bastard up at Command had a right fucking sense of humour. April fucking Fools Day. Prick.

We landed at dawn just on the other side of the river from Fort Rockcliffe and had to march to the place that Command had chosen for the battle, a little place called Monkhill, not Carlisle despite what they call the battle now.

We were silent the whole time as we didn't want to get the show started early and there were small teams of the Royal Scouts ranging ahead of the unit to silence any G's that might discover us. I tell you, those guys were fucking insane. They were made up of lads from the Special Forces, the military dog units and the Household Cavalry. It was their job to keep the Gs off a unit until it was ready to fight and then to slowly draw them in for the kill. It must have been physically and mentally knackering, running or riding around the Grey playing a fucked up game of Pied Piper with a load of Gs on your arse. I considered joining them for about a second but then remembered that I like having my mates standing either side of me behind a shield wall. Fuck running around with a dog and silenced rifle for a game of soldiers.

Anyway, we made it to an overgrown wheat field just outside Monkhill with clear fields of fire and began to dig in. It was standard procedure now to build defences whenever we stopped for the night or to fight a pitched battle. "Field fortifications" they called it; digging a bloody great square ditch is what I called it, I felt like a fucking Roman. We all dug our specific bit and then put our shields on top of the mound. These were a great bit of kit, a metal rectangle about three feet high that you could sling on your back on the march or set it in the ground with an angled spike to hold it up. It wouldn't stop a group of zombies but it would slow them down and it made you feel a whole lot better having a barrier between you and them.

About nine O'clock we were set and ready to go. The ditch and walls were built, the range markers had all been set out and everyone had eaten breakfast and had a chance to take a piss. The command group in the centre had set up their radios and the surveillance balloon was up on its tether. The call had gone out to the Scouts to begin reeling the Gs in and we could see them beginning to walk in over the fields with a tail of infected shuffling after them.

We all stood to as they got a thousand meters out and the Scouts came running back into the perimeter, at the same time the band began to play. The Pipes and Drums were banging away with Highland Cathedral. I remember being disappointed by the small numbers of Gs that were coming in, there must have only been something like two hundred and I thought that this will be over in a second.

Of course, that was when the rest of the bastards turned up, a huge wedge of grey that just piled over the brow of the far hill and came straight towards us. The Scouts must have pulled half of the Carlisle swarm on to us. That was when I suddenly needed a piss again but I looked either side of me at the lads and stood firm. The music helped, of course, it's hard to feel afraid when the pipes are playing, it really gets you going and I felt seven feet tall.

By the time the first G's got to the five-hundred-meter line, we were all like dogs straining at the leash with our teeth bared. It was like "come and fucking have some", the adrenaline was pumping and we were fucking ready to go.

At five hundred meters, the sharpshooters began to take down the leading G's and a line of corpses began to build up but they just kept coming, walking straight over their dead, arms outstretched coming for us. At four hundred the band stopped playing and ran to their positions in the centre of the square to act as our reserve. The Regimental Sergeant Major raised his voice and yelled "Battalion…. Kneel", the front rank knelt with the second rank standing behind us.

"Battalion....present ARMS! ", across the front rank, our SA80's came up to face the enemy. I looked through my sights at the target I had picked, some bloke in a business suit with half his jaw missing. I controlled my breathing and waited. As they crossed the three-hundred-meter line the order came to fire, I squeezed the trigger, felt the recoil and watched as the whole front of the horde just dropped like they had been cut down by a scythe.

After that it was just automatic, the base drum began its one-second beat and we fired on every thump just as we had been trained. I emptied my first magazine into the horde and just kept on going, change magazine, sight your target and keep firing to the beat of the drum. By now there was a barrier of corpses building up and they began to spread round to the flanks and that was when we heard the other lads open up.

I emptied my six magazines and stood up yelling "change" as the man behind me stepped forward and took my place. I raised my hand and one of the Powder Monkeys came running over, he was a young lad about fifteen and carrying a satchel full of magazines, we swapped empties for full and then he was off to the next guy. It was a good system as it meant each man got about three minutes to reload, take a drink of water or a quick bite of a power bar before getting back into it.

I remember taking a moment to look around and see how the battle was going; we were now fighting on three sides but seemed to be holding our own and a carpet of bodies seemed to be piling up between the three hundred and two hundred markers. The next time I remember looking around that carpet had become a mound that the bastards had to climb over to get to us. By then we were completely surrounded but despite the numbers against us, nothing had reached the hundred-meter marker.

At some point, I noticed that the rate of fire had slowed and that my breaks were getting longer. I looked around me and saw that we were completely surrounded by a wall of bodies about ten feet high and every now and then a G's head would appear over the top and get shot off. I glanced at my watch and realised that only three hours had passed since we had set up but we could already tell by the moaning from the other side of the wall that the numbers were starting to fall off. We were given the order for half the Battalion to stand down, so while half of us took a breather, cleaned our weapons or got a bite to eat the others stood on the line and took pot-shots at anything that moved. Amazingly some of the lads even managed to fall asleep.

A few hours later we could tell that it was almost over, there were less and less heads popping over the wall of bodies and the officers in the middle were looking at their computer screens and talking on the radio. By two in the afternoon it was all over, an armoured tractor had been airlifted into the square by a Chinook and bulldozed a path through the wall. The Scouts went first to clear out any stragglers but by then we were pretty confident that we had broken the chain. It was a weird feeling, standing in this totally silent field with a huge square of corpses as the only proof that we had even fought a battle here. Of course, that peace and quiet didn't last long as it was time for battlefield sanitation, you have to remember that at this time we didn't have the American PIE rounds yet, the ones that burn inside the brain and make clearing up much easier, we just had the old 5.56 NATO standard round and that made a fucking mess of the human head I can tell you. On top of that, we had to make sure that every one of the bastards in the mound was dead.

It was one of the shittest experiences of my life, talk about a comedown. Going from the high of having survived the first pitched battle of the Restoration to tossing bodies onto a huge bonfire that the engineers had built, fuck me that stunk. It got a bit hairy too, as some of the Gs were still alive. I guess they must have been trapped by their mates falling on top of them and now they came tumbling out, grabbing and biting. One of my lads almost got bitten but managed to get his cutlass in the way in time while his mate took the fucking thing's head off.

166

It was getting dark by the time we were finished and we packed up and marched to the boats, all I wanted to do at that point was get back to the fort, shower and sleep for a week. Of course, the first thing that happened after we finished cleaning our kit was we all went straight to the bar and got pissed. It was great; we all talked and joked and bigged ourselves up, competing with how many Gs we thought we had killed. It was typical soldier shit but it helped to burn off the last of the adrenaline and I suppose a lot of the stress and fear that would cause us issues further down the line.

Do you know that after the Falklands War there were fewer cases of PTSD in the Royal Marines than the Army? It was all because the Boot Necks went back by sea and had three months to talk through all the shit they went through rather than the Army lads who flew home and twenty-four hours later were kissing their wives and sweethearts. No wonder it fucked your head up.

The next day, with a lot of sore heads, we were paraded and told that we had killed over ten thousand zombies and achieved a great victory. Before we went back to our regiments we were all presented with a white piece of cloth with the words Carlisle stitched onto it and told to sow it onto our uniforms and wear it with pride. I guess there was not enough metal to spare to make any medals but I did wear it with pride and still do.

Jock points to his faded red coat hanging in a frame on the wall. There is a score of battle stripes on the right sleeve.

After that, it was back to our units and a few months later we were on the offensive. The Restoration had begun.

On the move

Department for Infrastructure, Whitehall, London.

Frank Elman is a former British Army Royal Engineer. Since the end of The War, he has been a senior manager in the Department for Infrastructure, responsible for the building and maintenance of the entire critical national infrastructure, from roads and rail to defensive walls and power stations.

Frank is responsible for the maintenance of the national defences and the transport links, a job he has much experience in, given that during The War he spent much of his time building the defensive walls that still criss-cross the nation.

During The War my main role was the construction of the defensive walls that divided the country into manageable chunks, sounds easy doesn't it but the reality was much more complicated. For starters, there was a supply problem. Did you know that the first thing an engineer does when they start a new project is to look at the plans and work out what resources they would need to complete it? Well, we took one look at the plan and just said "no way".

Why was it not possible?

Well, the plan in outline was to physically divide the country into sectors and then clear them inch by inch if we needed to. In order to do that the idea was to build blocking walls using the motorways as a guide. The problem was that we needed a hell of a lot of concrete walls to do it and we had nowhere near enough. I know everyone who was involved in the plan likes to give the Royal Engineers grief, say that we were like car mechanics sucking their teeth and saying "Oh, going to be expensive" but if it wasn't for the Ministry of Resources then I guarantee you that the plan would have never have left the Prince Regent's office.

As it was the Ministry pulled it out of the bag, Christ knows how but they found workers from somewhere, opened up three more concrete factories and worked their arses off to produce enough T-walls for us to start the first phase.

How did the actual building happen?

Thankfully we had already had a pretty good trial run when we did Op Euston and moved the Northern Defensive line from the Antonine Wall to along the A69. In that Op we had waited until the middle of winter, basically when the snows were at their heaviest and all the infected were frozen solid, then started building the wall outwards from three different points. The first team started at Newcastle and were by far and away the fastest as they had all their wall sections coming in by sea. The second team started at Carlisle and were almost as fast being supplied down the M6. My team were in the middle near Hexham and had to be supplied down the A68.

It was bloody hard going but by the time the first snows had started to melt and the Gs were twitching we had it finished; a great big bloody wall right across northern England to stop any of the moaning bastards from moving north. All of us Engineers legged it back behind the Antonine as soon as possible and left the poor infantry to sweep the land clear ready for the settlers and farmers coming up behind.

The Restoration was basically a carbon copy of the Euston plan. Build a wall in winter to section off part of the country and then let the infantry clear it. It was simple and effective as it meant that we weren't trying to fight the whole island at the same time. It got a lot easier as well once the country got into the swing of things. The civis would spend all spring and summer producing T-walls and then moving them either by sea, rail, road and even canals, to drop off sites ready for the winter build. By the time the troops hit London the whole thing was running like clockwork.

However as far as I am concerned the real genius of the plan was the contingency it put in place for the future.

What do you mean?

If you look at the detail of the plan it calls for the country to be divided up into manageable chunks, each sector would be further divided up by the fortified motorways that crossed that sector. All of this meant that in reality the whole of the country was divided up into very small areas that could be isolated from one another should an outbreak ever occur again in the future.

By implementing this plan Command had essentially put in place a nationwide redundancy to ensure that a national outbreak never happens again. If you look at it before The War there was no physical way of stopping a G from London walking all the way to Scotland; now it would walk straight into the M25 wall, or have been destroyed by the motorway patrol before it even got close.

It's the reason we spend millions of pounds today on things like urban defences, fortified motorways, hardened railways and all the troops and Militias to defend them. It's all in the name of redundancy, to seal off an infected area to prevent it contaminating the rest of the country.

I'm sure that in a few years we will all get lazy and complacent again and some politician or lobby group will start moaning about how expensive the defences are or how they are breaching people's rights to move freely and demand they be removed but until then I for one am glad they are there. The whole bloody war started because we weren't prepared for it and because no one saw the writing on the wall. Of course, the walls do help to keep me and several thousand people in a job.

North to South

Jock and I have retired to his living room and are currently enjoying some of the locally brewed whisky. Sadly, while it is not as good as any pre-war vintage it certainly has a kick and would I imagine keep a man warm on a cold South Atlantic night.

After Carlisle, my platoon and I were rotated back to the Scots Guards and from there it was just non-stop for a month. It was like walking into a madhouse, people were running around all over the place, the kit was being issued, lads and lasses were training on the ranges, all that sort of stuff. I had expected to come back to a hero's welcome and not to have to pay for a drink for ages but all we got was "Alright mate, where you been then?" It turns out that everyone had been shown the drone footage of the battle and had been fully briefed on the tactics. Now everyone was just in full on war mode and didn't have time to swing the lantern. Kind of took the wind out of my sails.

I found out from one of my mates that while we had been away prepping for Carlisle everyone else was doing the same thing. I guess the idea was that if the battle went well then the Army could just roll straight over the start line and get on with it and if it went badly then I guess Command would have chalked it up to experience and come up with a new plan. As it was the battle had been a great success and we had been given a month to get ourselves prepped and ready to go on the offensive.

I can't tell you how different the Army that crossed the Wall was to the one that I joined four years before. It really was an army of the people. Before The War there were all sorts of criteria for joining, things like there were no women in the infantry or cavalry, you had to be a certain age or a certain fitness level. There was none of that now if you could walk twenty miles in a day, fight a battle at the end of it and shoot straight, then you were in. Of course, everyone who was still alive had to have fought to stay that way which gave us a pretty good recruiting pool to draw from. In my unit I had men and women from all former walks of life; I had one guy who had been a millionaire music mogul, another girl who had been a "celebrity" on one of those reality TV shows. I guess it was one of the things about the war, it brought everyone down to the same level, almost like resetting society and everyone had to earn their place from the bottom up. All of our tactics had changed from the conventional warfighting to the stuff we trialled at Carlisle.

All of our equipment had changed. No more heavy as hell body armour or helmets. No more camouflage combat dress, after all, there was no point trying to hide from the Gs, we wanted them to see us and come straight for us. Instead, the Ministry of Resources had produced a new uniform for us.

It was actually pretty good considering it had been manufactured on the cheap from whatever the Government could lay its hands on, the main part was a two-piece combat uniform; navy blue trousers that had these clever little insert pockets on the knees and shins where you could put padding and bite plates, if the situation required it, and the now famous Red Coat.

It was a surprisingly good bit of kit, the guys who had designed it had clearly been reading up on their history as it was a dead ringer for the ones that soldiers wore at Waterloo. It was a deep scarlet red and was thick enough to keep you warm but not so much that you melted on a long march, it was pretty comfortable and had the same insert pockets at the trousers. The ones on the forearms were pretty clever as they were strong enough to use as a shield from a zombie bite. There were a couple of times on the march when those things saved my life, gave me enough time to jam my arm in a Gs gob and then smash its brains out with the cutlass. Most of the historians today reckon that the reason they chose to give us red coats was because of the historical significance, fighting for Britain that sort of thing. I guess that was part of it but the Army will tell you it is because red is easily identifiable on the battlefield which

172

meant you always knew where your mates were, it also meant that white rank stripes showed up nicely on your arm. The other reason is that red dye is also cheap and easy to produce. It is kind of comforting to know that some things really don't change; the Army is always supplied by the lowest bidder.

The best bit were the boots though, everyone had a pair of really solid and sturdy boots, I guess they knew that we would be walking the whole way so they spared no expense. They were comfortable and sturdy enough to stop a G taking a chunk out of your ankle. The rest of the kit was pretty simple, a black cloth cap for summers and a thick woollen one for winter, a heavy wool great coat for when it got really cold, a webbing belt with ammunition pouches and a water bottle and a rucksack for everything else. Our weapons were pretty standard as well, a cutlass and rifle for everyone, no machine guns, mortars or anything like that, just the standard infantry equipment regardless of rank or role.

What rifle did you use?

We still had pretty much the same weapon that we had before the war, the old SA80. Don't believe all that shit in the press from years ago about it being an unreliable weapon it was brilliant. Sure the old A1 was crappy and cheaply made, constantly jammed all that sort of stuff, but the A2 was a dream. If you want your weapon redesigned and fixed get a German engineer to do it and that is exactly what they did in the 90s. The version we had now was the A3, it was lighter, more robust and much more flexible. They had removed the fire selector so you could only fire on single shot, and the barrel had been made about three inches longer so you could get another hundred meters of range. They had kept the old foregrips from Afghanistan so that you could either hold the down-grip or flick out the collapsible bi-pod for a really stable shot. The foregrip also had this clever little bayonet that would telescope out if you needed it, truth be told it was pretty useless as you had to be pretty lucky to stick a zombie through the eye, it was much easier to shoot it in the face if it was that close or use your cutlass. The sight was pretty sweet too; it gave you a 4x magnification and allowed you to pull off headshots at 300m or allowed you to look over the sight if you were fighting in close quarters like a building or something. There were the ancillaries like the torch and laser dot, they were great when we started to clear buildings as you could use the laser to get snap headshots at pretty close ranges.

I love that rifle, it was reliable and solid in all the years I used it I never had one jam or misfire. I guess the old phrase of "if you look after your rifle it looks after you" is true.

How does it compare to the rifle the Americans used?

Look if you want to kill two hours between a couple of soldiers then ask them to compare guns. If you're asking which is better, I can't really say; the Yanks like to say that theirs is a custom made rifle which took the best designs from around the world but I say if it ain't broke then don't fix it. The SA80 was a good rifle and was made better with limited resources plus we didn't have to change the ammunition around. Sure the .22 PIE round was great for killing zombies but look at all the work the Americans are having to do now to retool their rifle to fire 5.56 now that it looks like we are back to good old human on human fighting.

So when did you get the order to move?

It was the beginning of May and we were moved to our start line at one of the gates in the north wall. The guys on the wall had spent all winter clearing a front about five miles deep so that we would not have to fight our way clear. The Engineers had spent all that time building the next wall along a line from the coast near Preston, to the outskirts of Manchester, to Leeds and then to the coast at Hull and all the fortified motorways in between.

When the order finally came to go, it was a real "hurry up and wait" situation. It took almost a week for the entire Army to get in line, there was lots of marching to our positions in the line and then waiting for other units to take their position, then for Command to check that everything was perfect, lots and lots of waiting. It's the worst part of any operation, it gives you time to think about all the shit that might happen, could happen, every single possible way things could go wrong. You can always tell the young and inexperienced ones from the veterans when you are waiting. The young ones fret and fidget, check their gear and weapons over and over. The veterans, they sleep because they know that you might as well sleep when you can, because once we start we are not stopping until winter.

So there we were, the entire army sitting in a line, two deep, that must have stretched from coast to coast. Two meters between each man and their neighbour and the Platoon Sergeants and Platoon Commanders patrolling the line to the rear and to the front. That was the great thing about the British Army, the officers always led from the front. Didn't matter if they were a young Lieutenant or a Colonel, they would always walk at the front of their men and be the first one to face the enemy. It led to a very high attrition rate, mainly through stress but it gave the soldiers behind them confidence and always steadied the line. Of course, it helped to have a big, scary sergeant behind you to stop anyone running away.

Finally, the order to march came; we kicked everyone onto their feet and then the officers started forward and the line followed. It was surreal, like watching one of those police searches, where they are looking for evidence. We walked at a steady, energy conserving pace that could cover about twenty miles a day, every now and then there would be a shout from one of the sergeants to dress the line, speed up or slow down but after a while most of us gave up. As long as you could see your neighbour then no G was going to get past.

The first few miles were easy as it had already been cleared but then we started to see the Gs, in ones and twos at first but in bigger and bigger groups as we got closer to urban areas.

How did you deal with them?

The lone Gs or the ones in small groups were easy. The line never stopped; not for bad weather, fog or rain, only at night, so we pretty much steamed straight over them. As soon as we saw them either the guys who were scouting ahead would take them out or if there were too many, an appropriate sized response would stop and deal with them. Once they were done they would mark the bodies with a small red flag so that the "Battlefield Sanitation" teams could burn them. We called them the BS teams as it was such a bullshit job but I am glad they did it, I really didn't want to. After they were done the guys would rejoin the line and crack on.

It was pretty easy at first. The ground was pretty open but then we started to hit more and more towns and cities and things got more interesting. Villages were pretty simple things to deal with; whichever part of the line got to them first would stop and surround it while the place was taken by one of the battalions in reserve. Then we would go in and clear it house by house. It was slow, tiring and frankly scary work as you never knew when a G was going to jump you. I'm making it sound like it was a big surprise whenever we came across a town but the truth is that we always knew what was coming and what the plan was. Command had their UAVs up ahead of the line, mapping the ground and giving them time to plan how many soldiers would be required for each site.

My battalion had it pretty easy as we were clearing a section that ran through the centre of the country between A1 and M6 fortifications, it was pretty sparse open country with lots of desolate farms, small villages and town. It was nowhere near as populated as the coastal strips so it took us a lot less time to reach the M62. By mid-summer, we were on the outskirts of Leeds and that was when things got interesting.

We didn't have enough troops to just march straight through the whole area and it was not like we could surround the city as no modern city has a recognisable edge, there was just a spread of houses, shops and industrial estates surrounding them and often spread into another cities border. Instead, we pretty much rolled out the tactics from Ireland and Carlisle. Each battalion came together for the first time in three months and dug in on the outskirts of the city, we had to do it fast as we were close enough to the city for any Gs nearby to see us and touch off a chain swarm. We dug in fast and within a few hours had a marching camp built and the surveillance balloon up. Then we waited for the other Battalions to dig in and for everyone to be ready. Finally, we got the word and stepped up to the wall, at the same time the bands started up and we could hear the bass drums rolling across the hills from us and the other positions nearby.

Evidently, the Gs heard it too and we started to see them emerging from the city, first in ones and twos but then in greater and greater numbers. Pretty soon there was a flood of Gs heading straight for us. After that, it was just business as usual as we cut them down, row after row of them. It was pretty easy going at first and I remember thinking that it would be like Carlisle and be over in a few hours but after four hours with no let-up, I started to get a bit concerned. After eight hours I was bricking it, certain we would be overrun or run out of ammunition but I didn't need to worry, it seems Command had planned for this and we had more than enough ammo and men to fire it.

Thank God for the other positions, they took a lot of the heat off us. Without them, we would have been overrun for sure. Twelve hours later it was over, the last few Gs were dealt with and we could finally have a rest. It took a week for the BS boys to clear their way through to us but in that time we had rested and were ready to go. Then it was into the city, a building by building, house by house and room by room search. Thankfully most of the Gs had been pulled out by the music but there were still those who had been trapped in homes or offices and it was those buggers we had to clear out. Problem was they weren't the only thing we had to deal with, there were lots of ways to get killed in those cities without getting bitten.

Such as?

Well, there were the Ferals for a start, both animal and human and I don't know which one was worse. The wild dogs were probably the easiest to find as they would always bark or growl when you got near but they were always in packs so you had to make sure you shot them all fast or they would tear you to pieces. I was clearing a house with some of my platoon when the floor gave way and one of the lads fell into a basement, he was a funny bastard always used to do impressions and make everyone laugh. We all looked into the hole and tried to find a way to pull him out but a pack of dogs was obviously making it their home and they were on him before we could blink, we shot them all but by then it was too late and he had been ripped to pieces. After that, we always shot first and asked questions later.

Feral cats were the worst, they were big, mean and cunning as fuck. They would lie in wait, up a tree or in the roof and wait for their prey to walk underneath before jumping out, this angry ball of fur and claws. I heard about too many guys losing their eyes to those fuckers. I hear they are still a problem today, all those cute hose pets just gone plain Darwinian, running around the countryside.

Feral humans were a different matter. Those were kids who had been abandoned when everyone else fucked off and somehow survived while surrounded by Gs. They were fast, strong, very clever and did not want to be caught. The official line was that we should try to capture them and only shoot to defend ourselves, that was much easier said than done. Those little bastards had been hiding for years so how the hell where we meant to find them? Often the only

178

way we did was when we accidentally walked into their territory and they jumped us. One guy must have been a kid about 18, he was so dirty he looked like Tarzan's ugly brother, jumped me as I was clearing a four-bedroom house, got me around the neck and was throttling me. It took four of the lads and lasses to pull him off and then another two to hold him down. We had to knock him out before we could hand him over to the Recovery Teams. After that, we all got really good at recognising the signs of a Feral's territory and avoiding it. We would mark it, report it in and then let the guys with the nets and tranquilliser guns go get them.

On top of all that, there was the damage to buildings; years of neglect, weather damage and often fire meant that even going inside one was a huge risk. I once saw a block of flats collapse because fire had warped the steel and concrete supports, no one was in it at the time but it made us all really careful.

There was the health risk as well, all those bodies, rotting food and stagnant water had made pretty much every built-up area a breeding ground for diseases. Things that we thought we had eradicated like Cholera, Typhus and Spanish flu had come back and hit us much harder because no one had an immunity to them anymore. There weren't even any stocks of vaccine because they had all be destroyed in the Panic. I heard of a couple of incidents where entire platoons or companies were quarantined because a couple of guys were sick. It really shook everyone up. Gs and Ferals you could fight, dangerous buildings you could avoid but plague, that you couldn't.

How long did it take you to clear Leeds?

It took about two months to go from our original base on the outskirts of town to the wall along the M62. We got there about a week before the first snows had started to fall and I thought that would be the end of it, you know, find a nice place to hole up and sleep through the winter. Did we bollocks? No sooner had the snows started and the first zombies frozen than we were up out in front of the wall clearing the ground ahead as much as possible. No, an easy thing to do through three feet of snow and ice, let me tell you. It's even worse when you see the bloody engineers driving past in their nice warm convoys to go and build the next series of walls further down. I suppose it is all fair though because as soon as it got really cold we were billeted behind the wall and left to rest while the engineers built the walls in the freezing cold. I say rest but we were really training up the new draft that had come out of the depots in Scotland and bringing our numbers back up to full strength.

What happened in the spring?

Actually, we were very lucky. The grand plan had called for a simultaneous break out from the North and South sectors; us to the Preston – Hull line and them from the Southern Zone, to a line through Gloucester, Swindon, Southampton and Portsmouth. They definitely had the easier time of it as they had less ground to cover and there where a hell of a lot less Gs since most of them had been drawn to the wall and destroyed over the last couple of years. They covered their ground in half the time that we did so they were dicked to clear Wales.

During the winter the engineers had been building a new wall which started in Chester, through Stoke on Trent, to the outskirts of Birmingham and then finishing in Gloucester. At the same time, Command had been moving units around drawing them from the north and south and positioning them along the wall for a push west to the sea. Once the snows started to melt they stepped off and cleared all the way to the Irish sea.

Meanwhile, I was left to stand sentry on the wall and fight off several million defrosted zombies that had come pouring out of Liverpool, Manchester and probably all the way from Nottingham. I am making it sound worse than it was; we were on top of a twelve-foot wall firing down on them, it was like shooting fish in a barrel, although there was a hell of a lot of fish. It was dull, and stressful because of all the bloody moaning but it was a really good idea and made the next year so much easier.

Why was that?

Well to the south of the wall were the Midlands. Before The War, it was one of the most densely populated parts of England and one of the most build up outside of London. Command knew that if we jumped straight into that in year two then we would be overwhelmed and killed. The Russians may have been able to afford thousands of dead but we couldn't. So we "prepared the battlefield" by pulling as many Gs to the wall as possible and then killing them. It was fucking boring but after a summer of shooting from the wall and a winter smashing those that were left we reckoned we had killed a good third of those in the Midlands.

After that it was back into the routine; Wales had been cleared and all available troops were in the line and then it was clear to the south.

The whole thing took two more years to get to London, first the clearance of the Midlands and Norfolk to the Gloucester – Milton Keynes – Ipswich line and then the Home Counties till we reached London. It was a hell of a journey and one that got more and more feral as we went south.

What do you mean feral?

Well, the areas further to the south had been abandoned the longest so had "returned to nature" as one of my soldiers put it. The whole place had become overgrown, with weeds and plants. It was amazing, really gave you an idea of what the place must have been like before humans turned up. Gardens and parks had overgrown, forests had spread and a whole new ecosystem had developed.

I remember clearing through Windsor Great Forest and thinking it was like something out of Lord of the Rings. Huge trees and deep black foliage, except with Gs instead of orcs. One of the real bastards was all the bamboo. Yeah, I know, who would have thought you would get a fucking bamboo jungle in England but there it was. All those ornamental shrubs that had been so popular before The War had just gone mad. There was no one to cut them back you see, so there I was hacking my way through a bamboo jungle in suburban Reading, fucking mad.

I know I am making the whole thing seem horrible and it was at times but there were some really great moments along the way. Linking up with one of the Burghs was always a good day, lots of flag lowering and saluting, that sort of crap but then a lot of drinking, telling stories, all the soldier stuff that goes on. The Settlements were a bit of a mixed bag though; sometimes you got cheering crowds and women throwing themselves at you but at others, you got resentment and anger. Never violence but just an undercurrent of betrayal that we had abandoned them, I can't blame them for it and I understand it but it was never a good feeling. Thank God we never had the problems the Yanks had with the secessionists or some of the Europeans with the criminal empires, we never had to fight and kill our own people.

The best one I ever took part in was the recapture of Windsor Castle. It had taken us four days to fight through the moat of Gs that surrounded the castle, there must have been millions of them pulled in from all over the place, but we eventually broke through. Throughout The War, the castle had been defended by the Coldstream Guards and the Household Cavalry who were both based in Windsor at the time, so there was a lot of ceremonial lowering of colours and a small Changing of the Guard ceremony.

Then we got to meet the Queen. She came out to greet us and thanked everyone who had taken part. She was really old by then and had to be pushed around in a wheelchair. She looked frail but she was still sharp as she joked and chatted with us. She died not soon after that, I guess it was all the strain she was under but it can't have helped losing her husband the year before and then her son in April that year. I guess that she hung on long enough to see her grandsons again and then passed quietly in her sleep.

We had her funeral in St George's Chapel in the Castle and I stood guard for her as she lay in state and all the political and military leadership filed past. It was one of the proudest moments of my life. Say what you like about the Royals before the war, when they were called to serve they stepped up, no ifs, no buts, they just got on with it for the good of the nation. Makes you fucking proud.

The King was crowned about the same time as the rest of the Army reached the M25 and began to build the wall that sealed London. That was really the beginning of the end for most of us.

London calling

General Palmerston has taken me to the Citadel, a monolithic concrete structure tacked onto the end of the Old Admiralty building. Built during World War II as a defence against Nazi invasion it now houses the Unclassified Operations room for the British and Commonwealth military. He shows me the huge wall mounted monitor that displays a map of the world with all of the current Commonwealth military operations as well as those of the UN and other world powers. What surprises me is the number of actions that are still taking place.

Depressing isn't it. When we hit the M25 we all thought this is it, The War is almost over. Back home for tea and medals. Who would have thought it would take so bloody long and that now a decade later we would still be conducting Ops all over the world trying to eradicate the last of these buggers.

Can you tell me about London?

All the battalions hit their marks at specific points on the M25 just as the first snows were starting to fall and after that, it became an engineering task. It was an incredible undertaking and they should be rightly proud of themselves. In four months, they had built their wall around the entire 117 miles of the motorway. By spring we had a twenty-foot concrete wall, built directly on top of the central reservation and barriers across all of the roads and bridges over the motorway. It was an incredible bit of work and gave us a four-lane road in the outside lane and then a nice clear killing ground on the London side. Of course, that was the easy part; now all we had to do was clear some 600 square miles of houses, offices, tower blocks, warehouses, shops and God knows how many miles of tunnels that run through the city. The job was made partially easier by the fact that a lot of central and eastern London was a burnt-out ruin but it was still a hell of a lot of ground to cover with a very limited number of troops.

How had you planned to take on this massive task?

Unfortunately, I cannot take any of the credit as it was not my plan. That rather thankless task was given to Major General Murray who had just been made General Officer Commanding (GOC) London. He decided we were going to take it nice and slow and damn what the media or the rest of the country thought about it. It didn't help that the previous summer the Americans had announced their impending offensive and were planning to steam roller over their country in their usual inimitable style but that was just not an option for the rest of us. We didn't have their manpower or their manufacturing base, the truth is that even with a third of the US controlled by the zombies the Americans could still produce more material and fighting soldiers than anywhere else in the world and I am not including Russian or China because just throwing men at the infected does not count as a sound strategy.

We all knew that everyone was expecting us to go in all guns blazing and be the first country in the world to be declared infection free, but look how well that worked out for everyone else who tried it. How many people did the Russians lose trying to take Moscow, or the French digging them out from under Paris, the Chinese in Beijing, the South Africans in Cape Town or the Brazilians in Rio? Mention any city in the world and there is a story of some bloody hard fighting and a long list of the fallen. We had no wish to lose any more people so it was "slow and steady" all the way, tortoise and the hare time.

The plan was broken into three stages. The first part was to take three months and consisted of what had now become standard practice. We put every single Battalion we had on the wall and as soon as the first snows started so did the music. It was the usual turkey shoot that had happened at every major city we had cleared only this time the soldiers had a lovely secure wall to stand on. I was in the Command

HQ at Luton Airport and watched the first few days via the feeds we were getting from the drones and balloons. We could see those infected closest to the wall start the whole thing off. As soon as we switched on the music that was it, we were reeling them in a chain swarm from miles away. You could follow it on the cameras, one of them would hear the music, turn towards it and moan and then the next one down the street would hear it and then the next and the next and so on. It was incredible. We had a team of scientists and doctors with us studying the footage and they observed one chain in an unbroken link all the way from the M1 gate to Regent's Park and that's when we realised we might have made a miscalculation in our planning.

How so?

Well, the plan was for us to lure as many infected as possible out of London to make the job of clearing it much easier when we had to go in on foot. The problem was we only wanted to pull in those that were outside the ring of the north and south circular. We were being far too successful and were starting to pull them in from central London. If that happened an area of the wall could have been breached and then we would have been in it neck deep. We turned off the music as soon as we realised but by then it was too late. There were just too many chains established by then and even though the lads and lasses on the wall were shooting them as soon as they appeared the firing just attracted more. We couldn't not shoot them as that would build up a moat around the wall that could create a breach, so we just had to grin and bear it and kill them as fast as we could. Everyone took their turn on the wall, even us in the command staff and something that was planned to take three months actually took around seven.

It was a bloody close-run thing and there were far too many moments when I thought a section of the wall was going to be overrun but some rapidly deployed reinforcements and some use of napalm helped to plug those gaps. In the end, though it did actually make the job easier as we estimated that we had pulled in over two million infected and it meant that the boys and girls on the ground had less to face when they went in.

Have you seen any of the pictures once the main fighting stopped, horrible isn't it, like something out of the killing fields of Cambodia? Just a carpet of bodies sometimes five or six deep, just horrible! Those poor buggers in the BS units had a hell of a hard time of it. None of them knew where to start, there were too many to try and bury and protocol said that we should burn them to destroy the virus so we just had to burn them in place. The bulldozers pushed them into mounds, lit them and then just kept piling them on. The smell was just horrific and we had to pull most of the units off the wall for the first two weeks just to give them a break from the smell. Those fires were still going at Christmas.

Still, there was no rest for the wicked and even though we had gone over our timeline we still had to try and reach the North-South Circular Line by Christmas but it was going to be pretty tight. I think I knew in the back of my mind that we were not going to make it but we had to try. It was early September when they went over the wall and the first snows were predicted to be a few weeks away but we had made the decision that we would not stop for winter this time. Of course, the winter helped us by freezing the infected in place but it did mean we had to go to them and clear them from every nook and cranny and that meant some difficult close in fighting.

In the good old conventional warfare days when humans killed humans, urban warfare was the one thing you always wanted to avoid. It sucks up manpower and spits out corpses. It is just such a complex 360-degree environment where you have to be constantly on your guard or you will be dead before you even knew it. Anyone who played one of the pre-war first-person shooter games can tell you that. In this war nothing had really changed; death could still get you before you knew it but instead of being long range with people shooting at one another from street corners or tower blocks this was all close quarters, bayonet and cutlass fighting. It was vicious, bloody and terrifying and even though a lot of the zombies had been frozen by the weather, there were enough of them in buildings or underground, protected from the cold, still mobile and ready to attack anything that came near them.

As I said before, we had made the decision to take it nice and slow and clear every single building no matter how long it took and it did take a long time. Despite having drawn in a lot of the mobile ones in the first phase, there were still all those trapped in buildings or locked in a basement by a well-meaning relative. It must have been bloody nerve-wracking for the soldiers on the ground, pushing open a door and not knowing what was on the other side. We realised very quickly that the biggest danger we faced wasn't the infected, it was the fear and mental damage that this kind of fighting created.

Within weeks we saw a spike in the number of suicide shootings, now that wasn't unusual in this sort of fight as a lot of soldiers who were bitten took their own lives if they couldn't make it back to an aid post in time for the euthanasia injection. But this was different, healthy soldiers were taking their own lives in increasing numbers and that was very worrying. We decided to rotate the units through the front, a week fighting and then two weeks at the rear relaxing and more importantly seeing the head doctors if they needed to. It slowed us down but we saw the number of deaths drop off dramatically.

By mid-November, the decision was made to push the Engineers forward to get started on the Inner Wall around the North and South Circular in preparation for the spring thaw. They got to work just as it started to get really cold. The poor buggers were out there in knee deep snow building the inner wall in one of the worst winters of The War but God love them they worked their arses off and managed to get the work done by early February. All of which meant the troops had a solid objective to work towards and that really helped to improve their mental states.

By March the troops had caught up with the Engineers and we decided to call a halt to proceedings to give everyone a break. So for a month, all the troops stood down and we treated them to some of the best food we could find, music shows and comedy acts. It was great fun and I think it really helped to relax some of the soldiers. We got some stick from the bean counters and armchair generals but we were vindicated when the shrinks reported that in the months after the stand down the number of suicides were down dramatically.

We got back on the offensive in April and again it was a very slow, steady and methodical advance but it ate up the miles and as the troops got closer to the centre of the city things sped up as more troops became available. By November we were nearing the end of the road, we were about two miles from Westminster but then the politicians got involved and decided they needed to make it a big event. We were ordered to halt and form a circle two miles from Westminster Bridge. It was all a big media event, they wanted us to advance together and have a big photo op as the first soldiers met on the bridge. It was a pain and a waste of time but I can understand why they wanted it. A big photo finish to be an icon of The War, like the Iwo Jima Marines or the Russians raising the flag over the Reichstag in World War II. Anyway, we did what the politicians asked, it took a couple of days to get everyone organised and caused no end of grumbling from the troops. What made it even more difficult was that we were still getting attacked from the infected left inside the cordon.

Anyway, it took two days but we were eventually ready to go, along with a veritable horde of journalists, politicians and other notables to watch and take part. Despite all my grumbling, it was a huge success, I am sure you have seen the images. The footage as the Scots Guards liberated Buckingham Palace and that sergeant meeting up with the leader of the survivors. The picture of the Prime Minister in the deserted House of Commons standing at the dispatch box and the most iconic one of the two soldiers meeting on

Westminster Bridge with Big Ben in the background. It was a great day made even more so when the PM declared Victory in Britain.

Of course, that was not the end of The War though. There was still a silent war going on underground and that showed no sign of ending anywhere near as quickly as the politicians would have liked.

Silent war

Westminster, London

Mike Hodgson and I have left the pub and are heading towards Westminster tube station. He is determined to show me the terrain that he fought through during the liberation of London.

For most of The War, I was part of the Royal Scouts. I'm sure you've heard the sort of things we got up to. Finding the swarms and them leading them on a bloody goose chase round half the countryside before we pulled them onto the guns of the Army. It was fucking scary work let me tell you, a small team of us, some dogs and a few silenced weapons playing pied fucking piper with some moaning bastards. But that was nothing compared to the work we were given when we hit the major cities.

Clearing the surface of a city was a piece of piss compared to trying to clear the bowels of one. God knows what people were thinking during the Panic but hundreds of them fled underground to try and escape the hordes and you know what, the infected just followed them straight down. The end result was thousands of the bastards wandering round in the dark beneath the cities and all of them had to be cleared out.

The first few subways that the Generals tried to clear were a fucking disaster. They tried to use regular troops, half of who had only joined the Army some six months before and here they were being shoved down a hole in the ground and being told to operate in tight claustrophobic conditions, pitch black with only your rifle's torch to light your way. Poor bastards must have been shitting themselves. The first Op in Newcastle when they tried to clear the Metro was a mess, they sent a Battalion into the tunnels and only a third of them came out. Poor bastards were ripped to pieces and those that escaped were so traumatised they point blank refused to go back in.

After that Command realised they needed a specialist unit to clear beneath the cities, and that is where we came in. They looked at the Royal Scouts and realised that all the ingredients were there already and they just needed a bit of reorganisation. The Scouts had been formed from all of the Special Forces regiments and some of the other specialist units in the Army, and Command just cherry-picked from all of them. The core of the unit was made up of lads from the SAS, made sense when you think about it, we were already trained to work in small teams in difficult environments, trained to use night vision goggles and silenced weapons, plus we had the mental strength to handle the stress of fighting in a tube line or a service tunnel. They attached some specialist troops, you know, dogs and their handlers, some engineers and when we needed them, some wreck divers from the SBS. God, they were some hard bastards. There is no way you could have gotten me down some flooded tunnel in the pitch black with only a spear gun and a shark suit for protection. No fucking way. Hats off to those lads, they were nuts and every single one of them deserves a VC for what they did.

Anyway, Command pulled us all together gave us the best equipment they could find, things like night vision goggles, IR torches to light our way, the best Comms we could dig up and silenced weapons so we wouldn't give ourselves away when we came across some Gs. We had about six weeks of training and then we were off.

Our first op was in Newcastle, thankfully they didn't have a massive underground network so it was a fairly simple task. We rolled up in our trucks and our new kit, feeling very sexy indeed. The Army had been ordered to hold at the entrance to each of the stations and had cleared out those Gs that had tried to get out at them, but the rest, those deeper into the station and tunnels, that was our job.

I was in charge of my team of six; four shooters including me, an engineer and a dog handler and his Jack Russell. That dog was a fucking miracle. It had been trained to sniff out the infected and then go stiff like a pointer. It was brilliant, saved our arses more times than I can remember by letting us know there was a G nearby or around the next corner. We were tasked with clearing the Haymarket station down to Gray Street station, while other teams were clearing other parts of the Metro and sewers.

We headed down the escalator with the shooters leading and as we got further down it got darker and darker as we lost the natural light coming from the street. By the time we hit the bottom and the main station concourse, it was dark as hell and I couldn't see more than five meters in front of me. We switched to NVGs and turned on the IR headlamps that lit up the scene. It was pretty grim down there with piles of bodies that had tumbled down the stairs. These were clearly the infected that had been trying to get out and had been gunned down by the soldiers at the top but as we got further in there were older bodies, some of them facing into the station. We guessed that these must have been the poor bastards who tried to escape down here during The Panic and been killed in the crush.

We split into pairs and began to sweep the station. It took a while but thankfully it turned out to be clear. We then formed up by the line that ran towards Grey Street and set off. That was when we started to get a bit twitchy. The IR light only stretched so far and beyond that the NVGs just couldn't reach. Looking back though, those tunnels were easy as hell compared to the shit we came across later, they were smooth concrete with very few service tunnels or alcoves which meant very few places to hide. Every now and then a G would appear out of the darkness and head straight for us. We would take it down quickly before it could call too many of its mates but we realised there was a bit of a flaw in the plan; you couldn't sneak up on a zombie. They could smell you or hear you or however the fuck they do it, well before we found them. Still, we managed to clear the line in about an hour with few mishaps and then turned around and cleared the tunnel going back the other way. By the time we emerged from Haymarket, three hours had passed but we had a much better understanding of how we were going to fight this war.

What happened after that Op?

After that, it was just straight into it for the entire war. We would roll from one city to another, clear it, write up what lessons we could learn, adjust our tactics and then move on to the next. By the time we hit London we had the process down to a fine art.

How did it work?

Well, the Army would clear the surface and every time they came across a sub-surface entrance they would cordon it off and shoot any Gs that tried to get out. It was a good start as it cleared the first few sections of the underground before we even arrived. Problem was we always turned up quite a while after the Army because we were tied up somewhere else. There were never enough of us to go around so we had a hell of a backlog to clear. It was a bit demoralising because we would turn up in our nice shiny trucks with our suits of armour and relieve a bunch of bored soldiers who just heckled us for being late. It was a pain but you just put your head down and got on with it.

Can you tell me about the armour, it was quite specialist, wasn't it?

It was a great bit of kit, the closest thing to Imperial Stormtrooper Armour I have ever seen outside of a video game. It consisted of a tight black body suit that had built-in temperature control. It would keep your core at the optimum temperature even if you were standing in a sauna and doing yoga. I don't think I broke a sweat once. That suit was covered by a flexible suite of segmented armour plates, it looked a lot like those suits of armour you see on Roman Legionaries, except ours was made of some Kevlar, thermoplastic material that was really light but incredibly

194

strong. The whole thing weighed less than 20 kg and could stop a Rottweiler from crushing your arm. It covered the whole body and all the vulnerable areas; forearms, shoulders, chest, legs and around the neck. The whole thing came with a full faced helmet, like a motorcycle helmet. It had a built-in air filter so you wouldn't choke on any gas build-ups or methane deposits. There was a night vision function on the visor with an IR torch, it had a built-in Comms system that used high powered signals that allowed teams to coordinate through concrete and the sector commander to triangulate your position. It was incredible and probably fucking expensive. God knows where they found them, built them or stole them from but thank fuck they did because they saved my arse more times than I can remember.

Anyway, we would turn up at a station or utility centre and clear an area down to the most defensible location. Often this was the station platform or something similar and then we would set up an operations centre. The bodies were cleared out, heavy lighting brought in, security, supplies and command staff. Then we went to work, teams spreading out through the tunnels and network and clearing the underground world section by section.

The radios were a Godsend as they meant that the officers who were running the whole thing could track our progress and map the tunnels as we went. I have no idea how they worked but they were brilliant. It meant that no one ever got lost and as soon as a team got a little too far ahead and started to lose comms the officers would set up another forward command location which had these cool radio boosters and meant we could push further and further forward.

By the time we finished in London, there was a whole network of command stations and resupply bases down there. You could live down there if you wanted to and we pretty much did. The War on the surface took what two years? I lived in those tunnels for pretty much three and a half years only coming up every three months to see what the fucking sun looked like. By the time we were finished, I looked like a G myself, all white skin and bloodshot eyes. If I had kids I would have scared the shit out of them.

What was the fighting in the tunnels like?

Well, it went in fits and starts. One moment you would be patrolling down a tube line or service tunnel all quiet and eerie then all of a sudden, a swarm of the bastards would just appear out of nowhere and we would be fighting for our lives. Sometimes it was long range and we had time to take them down before they got near us but most of the time they were on us before we could get a shot off and then it was all pistols, knives, trench axes and headbutts. Thank fuck for the armour, I am not joking when I say that stuff saved my life more times than I can count. If I ever meet the guys who made it, I will kiss every one of them and then buy them a drink. The armour plates were brilliant, you could jam your forearm in a Gs gob and it fixed them in place long enough to either blow its head off with your pistol or stab it in the brain. There were a couple of times when I got dragged to the ground and the neck plates and armour stopped me getting torn to pieces.

But that was how it went, moments of quiet with seconds of blind slashing, biting, adrenaline-fuelled terror. Day on, day off, with us only stopping to either set up a new forward base or be cycled back to the surface every three months for a week of rest.

What was the worst part of it?

There were two bits that I really hated. The first was sleeping. Whenever we needed to stop for sleep we had to find a secure place in the tunnels and just go firm and try to sleep. We couldn't go back to the closest supply base as it meant too much time lost going backwards and forward, so we slept where we could. We would find some hole in the tunnel or a service closet, barricade ourselves in as best as we could and then try to get as much sleep as possible. We would rotate sentry duty but with only six people in a team, it meant a lot of broken sleep. Every now and then a G would stumble on our position and the sentry would take them down. The first couple of times you woke up so fast only to realise that the guy on sentry had it all in hand. After a while, it became so routine that you slept through it all.

The second bit I hated was any time we hit a flooded section. If it was only partially flooded we would just crack on, hoping to Christ that nothing was going to grab you from below. If it was fully flooded, then we called in the divers. Those guys were all heroes. We called them Clankers because they always turned up on those hand powered carriages that you see in the old Western movies and they made a hell of a racket. Every time they turned up, we would be attacked by a shit load of Gs who had heard them. Always made things interesting.

Anyway, these guys would show up, kit up and then just jump straight into the flooded section. Just like that no goodbye or anything, just popped straight in and off they went with a shark suit and a spear gun. I hated the waiting you know, sitting there with your thumb up your arse not knowing if they were going to come out or if a G had got them. It was shit and you felt totally helpless. It wasn't like they were trying to clear the whole section by hand, most of the time they were just trying to locate the pumping system and get it unblocked or whatever.

Did you know that the entire central part of the London Underground is so deep that it is well below the water table and it takes a huge series of pumps just to keep the place dry? Of course, as soon as The Panic started the power died and the whole place flooded, trapping God knows how many poor bastards down there. One of the Clankers told me that he found this dry section in the Jubilee Line that was full of bodies, all of them whole but dry and desiccated like mummies. He thought that they must have been fleeing the rising water and been trapped before running out of air. Shit way to die.

Most of the time they would get the pipes clear or a fuse changed and then the water level would start to fall. Then it was really a race against time for the Clankers. They had to get out before the water dropped too low and the Gs were able to chase them. Most of the time they made it but sometimes they wouldn't and the next time we would see them was when we found what was left.

The worst times were when they made it part of the way out to only get pulled back in. One time we were helping to pull a Clanker out of the drink and I had him by the hand, about to yank him out when he suddenly fell back in. I thought he had just slipped and I called him a silly wanker but then I saw the fear in his eyes and realised he had been grabbed. I pulled as hard as I could but I couldn't get a good grip on the shark suit and he just slipped through my fingers an inch at a time, all of us pulling on one end and god knows how many Gs on the other pulling him back. As he disappeared under the water the last thing I saw was his pleading eyes through the mask so I pulled out my pistol and emptied the clip into where I hoped his head was.

It's what I would have wanted, that's how I justify it. Like I said I hated that part.

Combat like that fucks you up you know; your body becomes used to the adrenaline, addicted to it like a crack head. The combat, the nerves, fear and adrenal spike rewire your brain until you just become used to operating at such a keyed up level of tension that everything else seems mundane. The real problem is once the combat stops, it's like a drug addict suddenly going cold turkey. One day you are getting your daily dose of adrenaline, the next you have hit Westminster station and it is quite literally the end of the line; no more fighting, no more fear, just a pat on the back, a thank you very much for your valued service and now fuck off so we can get on with pretending that The War had in fact ended a year ago.

By the time I emerged into the real world, everything had changed; a nation was trying to come to terms with being at peace, the Army was abroad helping the Commonwealth sort themselves out, we had recaptured the Falklands, again, and we had crowned a King. On top of that, a lot of my mates were dead; of my team of forty, only twelve of us made it to the end. You try taking in all that and still stay level.

I became a very angry alcoholic, so did a lot of my mates and I spent far too much time getting into fights in pubs and then sleeping it off in a police cell. It got so bad that Director Special Forces, who was in the process of trying to reorganise all of the Regiments back to their Pre-War strengths, had to confine the whole lot of us to barracks for six months and subject us to a barrage of shrinks, therapy sessions and group hugs. It was a load of pink and fluffy crap but it worked, we all went in a bunch of head cases and came out as relatively balanced and professional soldiers.

BRITANNIA ASCENDANT

Post Victory Hangover

Grace Southerby is the current Foreign Secretary. For much of her life, she lived in Africa, the daughter of a career diplomat, living in what used to be Nigeria before The War started. She and her family were trapped in Lagos for much of the war, fighting and surviving on Lagos Island. During this time, she lost her father and mother to the outbreak and took the first steps on the road to the Foreign and Commonwealth Office when she fled to the small community on the island and led it to stability and security. She was eventually reunited with Britain when the first of the aid flotillas arrived in Lagos Harbour.

I have spent my entire life in the diplomatic world. As a little girl, I would attend diplomatic parties at various embassies and talk to the great and the good. My father would always sit me down afterwards and ask what I thought about so and so and if I thought they were trustworthy. For some reason, he trusted the intuition of a child over that of his seasoned staff.

The reason that I am telling you this is that I feel that I have had a very broad upbringing and have seen parts of the world that very few in government have ever heard of, let alone visited. This has given me a unique outlook on life which has served me well as a diplomat. There is nothing like spending a few years in a cut off hell hole to scrub you of your preconceptions of Britain's place in the world and another nation's view of you. That view, dare I say cynicism, is what got me to where I am today.

With Victory in Britain being declared in London, the country did what it did best, which is have a huge party but it was the wakeup call afterwards that was the real problem. It didn't take us long to see that there was still a hell of a task ahead of us. Much of the country was still in ruins, our industrial capability was limited to the two Safe Zones and most of the population was still stuck behind the walls of their Burghs and Settlements. We needed a plan to get back to a functioning economy and society. Fortunately, the PM had the foresight not to take the country off a war footing. As he said, "The job is only half done. The rest of the world is still in the grip of the infection and it is beholden on us to support our fellow humans wherever we may find them". Fine words but what did they mean in practice?

Amazingly, there was a plan. You will forgive my tone but politicians are not renowned for planning ahead and while I can't comment, as I was a few thousand miles away at the time, I am convinced that the plan was delivered by the military as a finished product.

What were the details of that plan?

It essentially called for recolonisation of the country. Despite best efforts during the Consolidation, we still had thousands of people in temporary accommodation and refugee ships all over the country and we needed to get them settled quickly. The Government established a settler council that identified viable locations, found the people with the right skills to make it a success and allocated the appropriate resources.

The result was like a second wave of the Restoration. Tens of thousands of people either headed back to their homes or found new ones. Farm collectives were established, recycling and manufacturing centres were set up and power and communication infrastructure developed. Thanks to vertical farming, renewable energy, 3D printing and bio-fuel harvesting, most settlements were self-sufficient within a year.

That was when we could look outwards to the wider world; the problem was that we didn't like what we saw.

Why was that?

Once again, the geography of Britain had been her saving grace. The Channel, the North Sea and the Irish Sea had been the most effective barrier that we could have wished for. Yes, we had hordes of refugees crossing by sea but that was nothing compared to the rest of the world. When all that is stopping the swarms of infected is a chain link fence and a line on a map, borders cease to be meaningful and the reality was that many of the nations of Old Europe and the rest of the world had just gone. Most of humanity was reduced to a series of fortified cities surrounded by a sea of infected.

One of the main issues we had was who to deal with. Europe was in a bloody mess and we had no idea who we should be talking to. The French still weren't talking to us after we blew up the Channel Tunnel, Germany and central Europe had fractured into dozens of small states, some of which were being run by old European royal families, some by warlords and one by a psychotic ex-prisoner who was running his own little kingdom. The Balkans had gone back to their favourite past time of killing each other; the Baltic states were just about clinging on despite God knows how many waves of infected coming out of Russia; and Russia was, well Russia. There was no way they were going to accept any help from anyone. The only people who were in as good a condition as the UK was the Nordic Confederacy and we already had a trade and defence agreement with them. **The Nordic Confederacy is a military and economic alliance of Norway, Sweden and Finland. It was formed in the late stages of the Panic to pool resources. Today it is one of the most successful alliances in history and is one of the major economic players on the world stage.**

So you see our problem. Back before The War an American President had asked "If I want to speak to Europe, who do I call?" now we were asking the same question.

What about the US and the UN?

What about them? The US was on the other side of the Atlantic, stuck behind the Rocky Mountains and in no position to help anyone. The UN was even worse; no seat of government, no real power or authority, at least not until VA Day. Only then did they get some clout when the Americans rallied behind them.

No, the way Britain saw it, we were an island of calm in a sea of chaos and we needed to start helping people pull themselves back from the brink.

How did you do that?

Well, the problem was that memories are long and Europe had always been a bone of contention for most Brits. Are we British or are we European? It is a question that has vexed politicians for generations and I still don't think that we have an answer.

Britain has always been a maritime nation, relying on trade and sea power to extend our influence and ensure we had the resources that we needed to thrive, so we resorted to type and looked outward beyond Europe to the old Commonwealth. But before that we did something even more in our national character, we invaded France.

Foothold

Calais has been a bone of contention between Britain and France for centuries. During the Hundred Years War, it was captured by the English and remained a crown possession until the 16th Century. It remained a political issue for many years following World War II, acting as a gateway to refugee traffic heading to Britain. During the war, Calais was overrun by the infected and abandoned. It was subsequently reoccupied by Britain as a gateway to mainland Europe. It is still a major political issue between Britain and France, one that the current mayor, Ian Hacker is all too aware.

So here we are again. A few hundred years later but once again the British are in France and we are refusing to leave. I understand the original reason for occupying the port and Calais-Nord, it was sound strategic logic but we are at the point where even I think that we have overstayed our welcome.

Can you explain the original aim for us being here?

The short version is that we needed a foothold in Europe from which we could deliver supplies and power to the rest of the continent. The long version is that when we looked over the Channel and all we could see was chaos, we felt that we needed to take matters into our own hands. The French Government in Rennes was refusing all offers of assistance from us and we needed a staging area that we could establish and then expand outward from, to deliver aid to isolated communities. Calais was the obvious choice. It was a short distance over the Channel, it was easily defendable and it had an existing port infrastructure. I think secretly some people also enjoyed the historical irony of us recapturing the last English possession in France.

How did the colonisation take place?

We don't call it that. It is "Liberation".

The Liberation then.

Well, it was a standard military operation. The Royal Navy cleared the underwater infected with their "ping and drop" and the Army flew in to clear the remainder. They established a perimeter wall around the port and old town and then the Engineers went to work clearing the port. That part took longer than the military operation, what with the hundreds of ships that had to be cleared and moved.

Once the port was clear, the dock workers, garrison, civilian administrators and staff arrived and started the business of establishing the port and building up supplies. An underwater power and fibre-optic line were run from Dover, the Channel Tunnel was cleared and that was it, we were up and running and in business. The problem was that we had no one to do business with.

What was the French view on all of this?

As I understand it, the French Government had no idea it was going on. It was only when the first Scout Teams began to reach isolated Settlements that they found out. They screamed bloody murder and threatened to drive us off but in reality, they didn't have the capacity. Ironically, it was only after they accepted our help and shipments began arriving in Brest that they could break out of their siege lines and start retaking territory. It did lead to a very tense standoff when the French Army closed on Calais and demanded that we hand it over. I think that it was only by some very clever diplomacy and the twenty-five-year lease plan, that we avoided all-out war.

How successful were the aid missions?

I think that they were very successful. The Settlements that we reached out to were more than grateful for any form of support and once the UK Government made the decision to give away plans for the vertical farms and 3D printing, Settlements could trade amongst each other. Pretty soon we had established a trade network of defended sites across most of Western Europe, it wasn't pretty and it wasn't formal but you can see how the Federation developed from it.

What do you say to the accusations that the British policy in Europe destroyed the European Union and the borders of Old Europe?

That is such a load of shit. Typical EU fantasist bollocks. Anyone could see that Old Europe was gone. Human control was limited to what could be defended and held. As one commentator put it "there is no peace beyond the line". In many cases that peace extended no further than the walls of your Settlement or if you were lucky some physical boundary like mountains or a river. Some were luckier than others though; Eastern Europe, Germany and France with their wide-open geography never had a chance. But look at the Swiss, they blew the tunnels and passes into the Alps as soon as they realised the danger and sat out The War in their typical style.

Yes, we indirectly helped to set up a series of independent and self-sufficient city-states that no longer looked to national identity. Did we intend to? No, but it was what was required at the time and on the plus side, it led to the European Federation being founded.

Commonwealth

The Foreign Secretary has brought me to the refurbished Foreign and Commonwealth Office which is the headquarters of the world's newest global power.

The Commonwealth was born out of our national need to do something to help the rest of the world. We had cleared our island ahead of pretty much anyone else, we were starting to get traction in Europe and we were now able to help anyone who wanted it. Of course, that was half the problem.

How so?

Well, look at our recent past. Three hundred years ago Britain ruled the world. I know that phrase will upset a few of your readers but that really makes my point for me. The British Empire dominated the world politically, economically, culturally and militarily. We were the superpower of the day.

We then spent the next one hundred years feeling guilty for it. Despite giving the world a common language, a common legal system, the industrial revolution and the abolition of slavery, all people remembered is that we conquered most of it at the point of a bayonet.

That was the problem we faced, no one was willing to accept our help; militarily that is, economically people were clawing at our door.

The need to survive as a nation meant that we had to innovate and adapt. Thanks to the work of the Ministry of Resources, Britain was now a world leader in hydroponic farming, renewable energy, 3D printing and algae biofuel production. On top of that, we still had the North Sea oil fields pumping away. In a few years, we had become a net exporter of food, energy and fuel; all that export had boosted the economy which in turn had kicked off the British manufacturing industry. We were still on a war footing, churning out guns and ammunition by the bucket load but we had started to produce everyday goods like clothes and medicines. Everyone wanted some part of what we were making and Britain was happy to donate or sell.

Did you know that Napoleon once referred to England as "a nation of shopkeepers", he meant it in a derogatory way but look how well that worked out for him? Ask anyone who knows anything; if you want to win a war it is usually the side that has the most money that comes out on top. And now here we were again, sitting pretty on a strong economy and a world that wanted what we had to sell.

And what were you selling?

Everything we could. Food, fuel, manufactured goods but what was really important was the knowledge we were selling; the technology and expertise as well as the military advice.

Was it successful?

Very, but not in the way we expected. Europe unsurprisingly wanted no military help of any sort. I think it was pride speaking, not that I blame them. If we were in their position I wouldn't have wanted some bloody pompous Brit asking if we needed a hand. Advice and supplies they were more than willing to accept but we made sure to limit military involvement to a few advisors and trainers.

We got a lot of interest from the old Commonwealth countries, but again they didn't want the British Army turning up on their doorstep, too many shadows of Empire. Not that we could have invaded anything anyway. After the VB Day declaration, most of the Army was demobilised and what was left was on its way to retake the British Overseas Territories. What they were asking for was advice, both technical and military and that was when the PM hit on the idea of the New Commonwealth.

It was based on the model of the Irish treaty and anyone who wanted our help could become part of a new international organisation that had at its core the values of free trade, military co-operation and a common code of laws. He called it "A political union of equals working together to make each other stronger." Admittedly it was a bit dictatorial of us to impose conditions on our help but I think history will prove the PM right. He saw an opportunity to build something great and he took it.

Many countries jumped at the chance to join once the offer had been made. Sign up to this charter of agreements and practices and you get a nice aid ship turning up at your door laden with food, fuel, ammunition and advisors. It was nation-building in a box and once everyone saw how successfully it worked in Freetown, everyone wanted to join. Most of the new African city-states joined as a block, followed by the Caribbean and Pacific islands. Canada, India, Australia and New Zealand were invited to join on account of their being in a much better shape than a lot of the world. After a hell of a lot of negotiation, they are now fully participating members.

It was a huge success. Today it is the most powerful trade and military alliance in the world and has been an incredible force for good. I know there are the commentators who say that the Commonwealth is a neo-colonial empire dominated by Britain but frankly anyone who thinks that does not have the faintest idea what they are talking about and has clearly never attended a meeting of the heads of state. Trust me there is no way I could dictate anything to them.

We knew when we were forming it, that there were certain areas that would cause issues. That is why the New Commonwealth Charter is so flexible. We dropped the bit about the Monarch being the head of the Commonwealth as that was always a touchy area, especially for Ireland and instead created a truly equal union. Every nation would have the same rights and standing as the others. There would be no president and each nation has a representative sitting on the council casting his or her vote. All decisions would be a majority rule and no one had the veto. We had learnt that lesson the hard way from watching the UN trying to get anything done. There is a single law code that all nations must enforce, it is based on English Common Law but as a lot of the nations were using this any way that was hardly a problem. However, enforcing it is, try getting some of the nations in the world to give equal rights to women or proper employment laws that don't allow exploitation of low-income workers. All I can say is thank God I am not a lawyer.

Economically, the Commonwealth has been a huge help to the world, by improving every member's infrastructure we helped to create islands of stability and production across the world that then acted as hubs from which more development could take place. It has helped to get economies and trade moving across the world and lifted so many people out of poverty.

Militarily it has really contributed as well. Once we trained up member states' armies to a sufficient standard they were able to crack on and clear their borders and then look to help their neighbours. That was always a slightly risky moment though, ensuring that one state did not cross the line from helping a neighbour to invading them. But we tended to find that the threat of an embargo was normally enough to stop any thoughts of expansion.

If you look at the Commonwealth now it is a major military player on the world stage. It is one of the largest contributors to UN operations and all member states have signed a mutual defence agreement, effectively ending the risk of state on state war in many parts of the world. Plus, slowly but surely, we are building one of the largest single defence forces the world has ever seen. It was one of the side effects of the training and assistance missions. Most Commonwealth states now have a common set of equipment and practices to work with and we are all starting to come together to build a truly international organisation.

To me, it is the perfect metaphor for how the world has come together.

When The Panic hit, every nation stood alone and we nearly all paid the price for that insular attitude. It may be a bit poetic of me, but I see the world as having been tempered by The War as one does steel. We all went through the fire and came out stronger the other side. Most nations are physically weaker than before but mentally and emotionally many are stronger than ever. Just look at Britain, before The War we had four separate national identities that caused no end of strife. But through shared struggle, we came together, broke down the old barriers and came together as a people.

I don't know what the future holds and I am sure that there will be some more conflicts along the way but I have faith that, as a species, we will take the punch that was the Zombie War, get up, dust ourselves off and move forward to make things better. If that sounds a bit twee than I hope that you will forgive me for having a little bit of hope that things will get better and we will learn from our mistakes.

Acknowledgements

This is traditionally the part of the book where the author thanks all of the people who contributed to the process and production of the novel. Instead, I would like to thank the process of writing itself as it gave me huge mental support at a difficult time of my life.

I first read Max Brooke's amazing World War Z novel while I was deployed in Baghdad in 2007 and it provided an amazing outlet during a testing time. I was always left with the niggling question of what else happened in Europe during this time, that was the first seed.

I later deployed to Afghanistan and in my spare hours started to write this novel. It was never meant to be anything more than a mental exercise to distract me from the realities of life on operations but on my return home, it became much more than that. The process of writing this book became a way for me to vent my frustrations at what I had experienced and seen others go through. More importantly, it was instrumental in helping me get myself back on track.

For all the parts of this story where I raged at the political process or seemed to glorify the military, that is purely a product of my personal experiences and not a political statement.

For all the parts that are unapologetically pro-British, I apologise for nothing. In Britain, we have a great tradition of being self-deprecating and talking ourselves down or lacking confidence. To this, I say we should take every opportunity to be proud of our history, of our people, our shared values and our potential as a people.

I would like to thank Max Brooke's for his amazing novel and providing the inspiration for this book. To George A Romero, the Godfather of the Zombie genre and the social and political commentary that they truly are.

Finally, thank you to my wife and children for the years of unconditional support and love but without whom I probably would have gotten this book written years ago.

Printed in Great Britain
by Amazon

23572444R00128